I

Conway

The undying past

THE UNDYING PAST

BY THE SAME AUTHOR:

Francesca
Dark Symmetry
The Abbot's House
Strange Visitor
Moment of Truth
Take Heed of Loving Me
A Link in the Chain
Dark Dream
Don't Shut Me Out
Cast a Long Shadow
A House Called Pleasance
Too Well Beloved

THE UNDYING PAST

Laura Conway

E. P. DUTTON · NEW YORK

First American edition published 1980 by E.P. Dutton, a Division of Elsevier-Dutton Publishing Company, New York

For information contact: E.P. Dutton, 2 Park Avenue, New York, N.Y. 10016

Library of Congress Catalog Card Number: 79-54042

ISBN: 0-525-22595-1
10 9 8 7 6 5 4 3 2 1

THE UNDYING PAST

✱ CHAPTER 1 ✱

The crowds milling outside Buckingham Palace were so dense that Rose Broughton, usually fearless to the point of indiscretion, clutched at her escort's arm and when he slid it around her protectively she was thankful, though she did glance over her shoulder wondering if her chaperon was frowning disapprovingly. But Mrs Talbot was not to be seen. The crowd had separated Rose from the austere widowed aunt to whom her parents had entrusted her, when rather surprisingly she had suggested to Rose that she should be her guest in London during Coronation week.

Rose had accepted rapturously, though truth to tell she had not expected to see much of the festivities. Mrs Talbot had made it clear in her letter of invitation that although she and Lavinia had received cards of invitation to attend the ceremony at Westminster Abbey, it would be impossible to procure one for Rose. She, perforce, would be obliged to stay at home, while her aunt and cousin departed in state. It could not be helped, and Rose, knowing that to her aunt she was no more than an unpolished country niece to whom because of Livvy's affection for her she was sometimes persuaded to be kind, had resigned herself to her background position. Even so, she would have a good deal to talk about and to boast about to her younger sisters, who were still in the schoolroom, when she returned to Derevale Manor.

But everything had turned out differently. Who could have supposed that on the eve of the young Queen's Coronation poor Livvy would fall ill with shivering fits and a raging headache necessitating rest in a darkened room, though she had protested so piteously against the doctor being called in that Mrs Talbot had given way to her over that. Grudgingly she had taken Rose instead of her daughter. They had driven to Westminster Abbey in Sir Rodney Perstyle's carriage. He, as Rose knew from an overheard conversation between her father and mother, was rumoured to be her aunt's persistent suitor. To a girl of eighteen it seemed ridiculous that such elderly people should think of marriage. Lady Talbot had been a widow for four or five years and was in her middle forties. Sir Rodney was considerably older. However, Rose's parents evidently considered it a very suitable arrangement. Sir Rodney was rich and Mrs Talbot was comparatively poor, for somewhat unaccountably her husband had left the bulk of his fortune to his daughter Lavinia who had only recently celebrated her twenty-first birthday.

Poor Livvy, thought Rose, it was sad that she should have missed this glittering day. Rose, being of much the same build, had been able to wear her cousin's pale-blue dress and white-satin pelisse and bonnet. None of her own clothes had been grand enough for the occasion. Afterwards they had dined at Sir Rodney's Mayfair house, a very elegant house, though he referred to it as a *pied-à-terre*. His estate where he lived for the greater part of the year was in Berkshire.

It had been a quiet, informal dinner, for the ladies had not returned to Mrs Talbot's Kensington home to change their gowns. The arrangement had been that they should sally forth to see the sights, as though, said Mrs Talbot, they were 'ordinary people'. Really, an absurd adventure, she had remarked, smiling indulgently, but the gentlemen had planned it and must not be disappointed, even though she was feeling quite anxious about her poor Lavinia, alone and miserable with her sick headache.

'But she begged you not to worry,' Rose had reminded her aunt. 'She said she would get well all the quicker if she had a long, long sleep with nobody to disturb her.'

It was only perfunctorily that she could make herself think of the afflicted Livvy, for this was a day beyond compare. The old Abbey had looked so strikingly beautiful, quite different in aspect from the historic building she had visited the year before when the family had stayed in London for a few weeks and a governess had escorted Rose and her sisters on an educational round of sightseeing.

They had had very good seats, and Rose had seen the young Queen, with no need to crane her neck or strain her eyes. She had been deeply impressed by the small, slender girl's dignity and composure. She had seemed so alone, though she was the centre of the brilliant pageant, her childish form bowed down by the heavy robes of state and the crown and regalia. Rose was not the only spectator with tears in her eyes and a lump in her throat. But the tears had not fallen, for she had chanced to glance sideways at Mr Tresham who stood beside her, and he had been gazing down at her with a comical expression as though the general emotion was uncalled for. She had smiled back at him, and he had said in a very low voice: 'That's better. Make no mistake, Vicky is a self-important little puss, and she's enjoying every moment of this.'

And why shouldn't she? thought Rose with some indignation. But she had understood what he had intended to convey. The young Queen was far from being helpless and overwhelmed; in reality she was immensely pleased with herself.

Rose was flattered by the hint of conspiracy in Mr Tresham's manner, but then he *had* been subtly flattering from their first meeting at her aunt's house. She did not deceive herself that he was romantically attracted to her, he was too evidently taken by Lavinia, who was an outstanding beauty. But yet he was intrigued by Rose, or more probably by her background.

Although she was shrewd enough to suspect that, she could not imagine why. Her home and her life in the country were sufficiently prosaic; but having discovered either from Mrs Talbot or Lavinia that her father was Squire Broughton of Derevale Manor, he had adroitly questioned her; not only about her ancestral home, but about the land her father owned on which stood the burnt-out ruins of what had once been the house called Pleasance.

Puzzled, Rose had asked questions in her turn, and Ives Tresham had owned that long ago he had heard of the old house and had never forgotten the description of it. That was all he had seemed inclined to tell Rose, and she was not particularly interested, though she *was* decidedly interested in Mr Tresham.

At the Abbey she had gazed around on many handsome men, but there were none in her opinion who outshone Ives. The court dress was romantic, and gave the wearers a distinction they might otherwise have lacked, but Ives, she thought, would have looked distinguished in fustian. The women could not help but look beautiful since the majority of them wore gorgeous dresses and glittered with jewels.

The little Queen, though extremely graceful, was plain but her train-bearers were lovely girls and the more enchanting for their rose-sprinkled, white-satin gowns. Rose wondered what they were all doing now, and imaginatively pictured them dancing holes in their satin slippers at some grand ball. Perhaps the young Queen was giving one. She would have been vastly surprised, and in spite of Mr Tresham's cynicism would have thought it pathetic had she known that the Coronation ceremony over, the Queen had returned to Buckingham Palace to give her pet spaniel, Dash, a bath and had then attended an exceedingly dull family dinner. At the present moment she was standing alone on the balcony outside the Duchess of Kent's bedroom watching the fireworks, while her exhausted mother slept and one by one the lights were extinguished in the Palace.

But now Mr Tresham, with Rose on his arm, was shouldering a way through the crowd. The rowdier elements were in the ascendant, but Mr Tresham was tall and broad-shouldered, and he had an air of authority. People fell aside for him, giving a clear passage. Rose admired his decisive manner, though she knew Lavinia disliked it, and said he was really too conceited. She was even affronted because Mr Tresham openly showed that he admired her. She could not imagine what people saw in him; he had so little polish, a defect for which, said Lavinia, no amount of money could atone. He was immensely rich, their distant cousin from Virginia, but nevertheless a nobody. His father had been the ne'er-do-well of the family, and had been shipped abroad with the hope that he might do better there, which in some mysterious fashion he had, with the result that years later Ives Tresham, an only son, had returned to England with a fortune.

In an intermittent fashion, Ives's father had kept in touch with his English connections, and on his death his heir had sold his estates in Virginia. Having found a letter written to his father by Mrs Talbot gratefully acknowledging his condolences on her husband's death, Ives had made bold on his arrival in London to wait upon her. Mrs Talbot had been greatly taken with him; not so Lavinia. That, Rose guessed, was a disappointment to her aunt. She would have been delighted had they made a match of it. 'Though we have nothing in the world in common,' Lavinia had told Rose disdainfully, 'and surely I have money enough, and am not obliged to marry for it. Ives Tresham is over thirty – too old for me. I detest his odd accent, and besides he has no ear for music.' And as though that settled the matter, Livvy had flounced away to her singing lesson, given by the fair, willowy, handsome young master who called twice a week to instruct her.

As Rose was not musical, that lack in Ives Tresham did not, so far as she was concerned, impair his attraction. She listened with no particular pleasure to Lavinia's sentimental trillings, and concluded that she was rather a goose. Lavinia being fair and tall and very slender had a sisterly likeness to young Mr Swan, the singing master. She was much admired in London society. Not so Rose, who was said to have a pleasant appearance – this patronizingly. She was as tall as her cousin, but much more robust. Lavinia's satin dress was somewhat strained across Rose's bosom, and tight under the arms. She had plentiful red-gold hair, but her nose was a snub, and her mouth wide; moreover she had freckles which sadly afflicted her. Nothing would ever take them away. Buttermilk, said to be a certain cure and liberally daubed on her cheeks and nose at bed-time, had no effect whatsoever.

Inconsequent reflections such as these loitered rather than flashed through Rose's mind as she was drawn through the crowd to the spot where the carriage waited. Her aunt and Sir Rodney were already seated there, and Mrs Talbot said irritably that she could not imagine how it was they had become separated. They had been only a few yards from the carriage, where they had a good view of the illuminations; and then, most unaccountably, Ives and Rose had been missing.

That was her fault, Rose knew. She had wanted a better view of the Palace and had said so. She had fancied that the little Queen might show herself on the front balcony; but no sooner were they within sight of the front gates than the lights in the Palace were dimmed, and they had been unpleasantly pushed around by other spectators.

'Which was no more than you deserved,' said her aunt tartly, when Rose, blithely unconcerned, had volunteered this explanation. She thought, as more than once before, that Rose was far too forward, and that her brilliant hair made her conspicuous. Really, it was a most peculiar colour.

Fortunately, a dark cloak put into the carriage with forethought, now covered Rose's Coronation finery, or she would have looked a figure of fun. It had been necessary for her to wear Lavinia's gown and pelisse, but none the less Mrs Talbot was resentful – perhaps because they suited Rose so well.

'It is late – far too late. We should be at home. Poor Livvy will be feeling neglected,' she said.

Sir Rodney accompanied them in the carriage to Kensington but Ives, who had bachelor apartments near Hyde Park, took his leave of them and said he would walk home. Mrs Talbot was pacified by the warm messages he begged her to convey to Lavinia. She had been sadly missed. He trusted that by the morrow she would be recovered, and he hoped he might be allowed to call.

Mrs Talbot gave gracious permission and on the homeward drive she disregarded Rose's presence and spoke freely to Sir Rodney of her hopes for her daughter. At twenty-one, she said, it was quite time Livvy was married. She had refused several eligible suitors, as much out of shyness as from any other reason, her mother believed. Vexing at the time, but now Mrs Talbot was confident that Ives's persistence would win her. 'I have never seen any gentleman more *épris*,' said Mrs Talbot.

Sir Rodney listened and agreed. Although sixty at the least he was still a good-looking man, rather like Lord Melbourne, thought Rose, who that day had gazed with such devotion at the little Queen Victoria. She realized that the – to her – elderly couple were indeed in love, and therefore the more anxious that Lavinia should become engaged to be married. Sir Rodney had no desire to accommodate a step-daughter at his London *pied-à-terre*, nor at his country home. Mrs Talbot, though she loved Lavinia and was ambitious for her, would be happier in her second marriage if her daughter was suitably settled before it took place.

The conversation floated over Rose's head, and she only dreamily absorbed parts of it. Sir Rodney asked questions about Ives Tresham. How was it that he had sold his plantation in Virginia and had come back to England? He smiled and murmured 'a romantic then', when Mrs Talbot told him that Ives had always felt that England was his real home. His plan was to buy an estate here. 'He disapproves so strongly of the slavery in America. How can one wonder at it?' Mrs Talbot said, and added something which Rose did not understand about poor Ives's father being a really dreadful person. 'He married a Virginia heiress, but that wasn't enough for him. He dealt in them, you know, made enormous profits so I understand. And then his poor wife died – of a broken heart so I've heard, for it was a most unhappy marriage, and afterwards there was this mulatto creature – though indeed I should not mention anything so improper, especially as Ives merely hinted . . . but when his father died, it was natural for him to want to sell out and get right away.'

They arrived at the house at last. The footman dismounted to open the carriage door. Sir Rodney bent low over Mrs Talbot's hand. In the light from the street lamp Rose saw the colour rise in her aunt's cheeks, and was surprised by the sudden sweetness of her smile.

They entered the house, with Mrs Talbot in a softened mood. She said: 'We won't wake dear Livvy, as it is so late. Tomorrow you can tell her all about this wonderful day. You have enjoyed it, I hope.'

'Enjoyed! Oh, more than that, Aunt Hilda. I shall remember it as long as I live.'

'There are some such days in everyone's life, my dear.'

'I can't thank you enough. It was too bad about Livvy though,' added Rose perfunctorily.

'Ah well! She will be glad to know you have been so happy. Livvy is exceptionally fond of you.' Mrs Talbot bent forward to kiss her niece's cheek. Each with a lighted candle in their hand they went up the stairs and separated on the landing.

There was a glance for Lavinia's closed door. 'She must be sleeping, the dear child, or she would have called out,' said Mrs Talbot.

Rose was very tired, but for a while the press of her thoughts kept her awake. She sipped at the glass of milk which had been left by a maid beside her bed, and nibbled at one of the sugared biscuits on the plate near it. The events of the day passed before her in a pageant of pictures. The light falling on the Queen's smooth head, on the jewels in her heavy crown; the exquisite grace of her floating walk; the broad strength of Ives Tresham's shoulder as it had pressed against her own – not intentionally of course, but because of the surge of people; the smile which narrowed his dark eyes, his thick, black hair. How *could* Livvy not admire him?

Recalling the snatches of conversation in the carriage on its homeward way, Rose wondered if she would ever hear the whole story of his life. It seemed unlikely. He might marry Livvy or he might not, but it would make little difference to her. The day after tomorrow she would be returning to her country home and in all probability would seldom if ever see him again. He was the most attractive and interesting man she had ever met, very unlike the somewhat uncouth sons of the farming squires who were her father's friends. Their freely expressed admiration was tedious to her.

Ives Tresham had been kind to her. He had liked her, even though he might be in love with Lavinia. At the oval dinner-table in Sir Rodney's house, they had been placed next to each other. He had peeled an orange for her, and she had been fascinated by the dexterity of his lean brown fingers as they manipulated the silver fruit-knife. The entire peel of the orange had come away in one swirl, not in small, clumsy pieces.

Yes – he liked her, but nothing more. She hadn't the remotest chance of getting him for herself, even though Livvy did not want him. Rose sighed, and at last blew out the candle.

❋ CHAPTER 2 ❋

As he had promised, Ives Tresham called at the Kensington house the next afternoon; but it was to find chaos and distress. A distracted looking maid admitted him, and while he stood in the drawing-room, puzzled by her long sideways glance, the door opened and Rose came in. She was alone and looked even more distracted than the maid.

'I am so sorry . . . my aunt is resting. She was – is greatly disturbed, quite ill. The doctor has been with her . . . he has given her something . . .'

Rose's lips were trembling. Nothing could make her look less than splendidly healthy, but her fresh colour had dimmed. Ives put his hand on her arm and induced her to sit down. Except for the short while when they had been alone in the crowd the evening before, there were always others present. Mrs Talbot's niece as well as her daughter was sedulously chaperoned.

'Why, what is wrong?' he asked. 'Is it – can it be Lavinia?'

Rose swallowed nervously. Her burnished head was lowered. She would not look at him.

'Yes – yes, it is,' she murmured.

'She is not – seriously ill?'

'Oh, no!'

'Then what is it?'

The bright head was raised. Rose blurted out in anger: 'It isn't fair that I should have to tell you, but there's nobody else. At least Aunt Hilda is sleeping. This morning I thought – I really did think she would go out of her mind. Oh, it's too bad of Livvy. She might at least have been straightforward about it. Nobody could have prevented her, for she's of age, but I suppose she thought there would be such a *scene,* and of course there would have been. Still to treat her mother so dreadfully, not caring what she suffered – the grief, the humiliation . . .'

'What has Lavinia done?'

It seemed that Rose could not bring herself to answer this direct question. She said, 'Such a hateful pretence, taking us all in. Aunt Hilda was worried about her all day, thinking of her left at home with a headache. But it was just an excuse to stay behind. She had the whole day to herself.'

'Why did she want a day to herself?'

The tautness of Ives's voice intimidated Rose, but at the same time angered her. Why should he care for Livvy, who wasn't worth it? She gave a sideways glance at him. He was biting his lower lip.

'To elope,' said Rose.

'Ah!' There was a perceptible pause before he asked: 'With whom?'

'Of all people that girlish looking Mr Swan – her singing master. They're far away by now. They got a good start, so there's no use looking like that, as though you wished you could challenge him to a duel.'

'Duels are no longer permissible, and were always uncivilized. What good would it do me to run him through with a sword or shoot him down? Even in an earlier age I should have had no legitimate cause. Lavinia and I were not betrothed.'

'But you loved her,' said Rose, and did not shrink from the angry gaze he turned upon her.

The anger slowly waned as he scanned her ingenuous face. He leant back in his chair and the tension eased. He said with a smile, twisted as it seemed in self-derision: 'I was fool enough to imagine it. Your cousin, Miss Broughton, is a singularly beautiful young woman.'

'So people say.' Rose was deliberately grudging.

'However, I shall not break my heart over a love-affair in embryo,' said Ives.

'That is very sensible of you.' The brisk patronage evoked a smothered laugh from him, and in resentful protest she said: 'Well, a great deal of nonsense is talked about love and broken hearts.'

'I agree. Tell me, when was it discovered that Lavinia had made off with this – er – whelp? I suppose you are certain it is Swan?'

'Oh, yes! She left a note.'

'Affixed to her pin-cushion?'

'How did you guess?' Rose was naïvely astonished. 'It was – with a long bonnet-pin. As it was late last night when we got home, and as Livvy's door was closed, Aunt Hilda thought it better not to disturb her. Then, this morning, when the maid took Livvy a cup of tea, it was found that her bed had not been slept in, and the room was empty. Of course Aunt Hilda had to be told and given the note Livvy had left, addressed to her. She wrote that she and Mr Swan loved each other, and had for ages. They had made arrangements to cross the Channel – to go to Paris, and they left here yesterday afternoon. The servants had gone out to see the decorations; Livvy sent word to them that they had her permission. When all was clear, Mr Swan – his name is Joseph – must have called for her. She took only hand-luggage with her, all her dresses are still hanging in the wardrobe; but of course she has plenty of money to get more. Poor Aunt Hilda, there is nothing she can do, though she did think of following them, or of asking Sir Rodney to go after them.'

Ives said: 'That would be useless as your cousin is of age. Mrs Talbot can only make the best of it. One thing is that whether Swan loves her or is no more than a fortune hunter, he will certainly marry her. Her reputation at least is secure.'

'I don't think he's a fortune hunter,' said Rose. 'I expect he's in love with her, though he mightn't have risked eloping if there had been no money. A singing master cannot have much of his own, can he?'

'One would think not.'

Rose observed thoughtfully: 'Aunt Hilda may not mind so dreadfully when she has got used to it. I mean – naturally she would have preferred Livvy's husband to be you, but she won't think of it too much if they make their home in Paris, and Livvy will be out of her way when she marries Sir Rodney, which will be an advantage to them.'

Ives laughed aloud. 'Really, Miss Broughton, I had no idea you were such a cynic.'

'Am I? It sounds rather horrid, but really it only means I am accustomed to say what I think.'

'A disconcerting custom in London society. Don't look so put about, for I assure you that I, at least, find it refreshing.

Now tell me, is your poor aunt really soundly asleep?'

'Oh, yes. Didn't I tell you the doctor gave her something – drops in a glass of water? I expect it was laudanum. He said she would sleep the clock round and feel much better when she awoke.'

'That being so, what is to prevent us enjoying an excursion on this fine afternoon? It's the first day of the Coronation Fair in Hyde Park. Would you not like to see it?'

Involuntarily Rose clasped her hands together. 'Oh, yes indeed, but it would be highly indecorous, and besides . . .'

'Besides?'

'Mr Tresham, you should be all sighs and gloom. I thought you would rush out of the house, and shut yourself away – mourning for her, and that the next we heard you would have gone abroad – far away – beyond Europe to shoot big game.'

'But my dear Miss Broughton, I am but an indifferent shot; the big game would be more likely to finish me off.'

'That,' said Rose with a giggle, 'would be a pity!'

Her eyes, bright blue and merry, twinkled at him; her wide, ripe mouth broke into a smile. She was an engaging creature, thought Ives, though utterly unlike the alluring Lavinia with her grace and fragility and large brown eyes which were so meltingly soft. He could have adored Livvy, he reflected, though aware that she was not equally attracted to him, he had held his emotions in check. Rose, on the contrary, was openly admiring, and with her youthful ingenuousness she was an amusing companion.

There was little difficulty in persuading her to accompany him that afternoon. She ran upstairs to put on her bonnet and a light wrap, and hoped as she gazed into her mirror that she would not look dowdy in clothes made by a country dressmaker after her festive appearance the day before in borrowed finery. Her muslin dress was fresh, however, and trimmed with pink ribbons which matched those in her bonnet. Her light cape and gloves were of pale grey. In spite of all the upset of the day, he spirits rose in a gay expectancy.

Rose had been to many a country fair, but these bore only a crude resemblance to the magnificent fête now staged in Hyde Park. On this bright June afternoon there were sight-seers and merrymakers in plenty, but they were more decorous than those who would swarm to the Park after working hours, when the darkness would be penetrated by thousands of fairy-lights strung on the trees. Rose was entranced, and regretted that there were so many side-shows, she could not see the half of them. Ives, in indulgent amusement at first, but afterwards infected by her tireless enthusiasm, gratified most of her curiosities.

There were halls of distorting mirrors which caused shrieks of laughter, but Rose turned away from them with a grimace. It did not amuse her to see herself and her companion as grotesques, either squat or elongated. The squat effect was the worst, for she had a secret fear that one day she might become horribly fat. Even at eighteen she was plump, and the elegant Lavinia had said critically that she ought not to eat chocolates and creams and pastry but to content herself with fruit and lean meat and milkless, sugarless tea and coffee. Rose had no intention of practising such self-denial, though she envied Lavinia her slender arms, graceful, sloping shoulders and narrow waist.

The haunted house side-show was the most thrilling; eerie in its semi-darkness, with long, winding passages, skeletons which leered from unexpected alcoves, and sighs and groans, sometimes seeming to come from the roof and sometimes from underground caverns. Rose laughed and shuddered and uttered terrified cries and clung to Ives's arm which presently slid around her waist and held her closely. That, of course, was reprehensible, but other couples were similarly enlaced, and there was nobody to observe it when Ives stooped his head and lightly pressed his lips to her cheek.

By the time they were once more in the open air Rose was blushing, and she avoided looking at him. Feeling confused and self-conscious she went from stall to stall, exclaiming over pretty trifles displayed there. Ives insisted on buying her a profusion of fairings. Sweets in a silver net bag tied with ribbons; a gilded gingerbread cat; a small, tinkling musical box; a lace handkerchief and a white stick called a tickler, because at the top of it there was a cascade of many-coloured, paper streamers.

The band was playing with deafening loudness, and Ives pretended not to hear her as he examined a pair of pink-satin garters, ornamented with pearl beads. Giggling and protesting, Rose dragged him away by the arm. The other fairings were all very well, and she could give some of them to her younger sisters, but her mother would be horrified if she ever caught sight of pink-satin garters.

By that time Rose was looking slightly dishevelled. She was aware of it as she caught sight of herself in the mirror-glass of which one stall was composed. Beneath her chip-straw bonnet, her hair was straying in wisps, her face was brilliantly flushed, her dress rumpled. Mama, could she see her now, which thank heaven was impossible, would be shocked, but then this entire excursion was slightly shocking, and she prayed that her aunt would never come to hear of it. She probably wouldn't, for Ives had slid a gold coin into the hand of the maid who had been in the hall to open the front door when Rose had sailed down the stairs to join him.

They visited the skittles alley, and Rose with beginner's luck won a wax doll, dressed to represent Queen Victoria, in a low-cut silk gown with a tinsel crown on her head. They watched tumblers and clowns, and children dancing round the huge maypole wreathed with garlands and dangling ribbons. The vendor of a scent-stall sprayed Rose with a delicious perfume, and Ives bought her a large bottle of it. His arms were so loaded with purchases that Rose could no longer hang upon him, which was perhaps responsible for the distressing incident that occurred when they, at last satiated with sight-seeing, made their way towards the nearest park gates.

Here there were fewer people and they were not constantly jostled, but at the sound of raucous cries, Rose stopped still, and then before Ives could prevent her, pressed forward in irrepressible curiosity.

Two tawdrily dressed women were facing each other, shrilling abuse. They were encircled by rough-looking men, who egged them on with applause and laughter. As Rose gazed wide-eyed, the blowsier of the two women shot out a hefty arm and with clenched knuckles struck the other between the eyes. The victim yelled and flung herself forward to retaliate, and in the split-second before Ives realized what was about to happen, Rose was between the two viragos, attempting to separate them.

'Cowards – shame on you!' she cried, addressing the grinning spectators, and within minutes was herself the object of the attack. Down she went on the dusty grass. Her muslin dress was ripped and torn; a heavy blow landed in the small of her back. Her bonnet was pulled off, and her bright hair cascaded over her shoulders.

There was the sound of a police whistle, and in an instant the small crowd dissolved and scattered. By the time two running constables appeared in sight, Ives had lifted the only half-conscious Rose in his arms. The fairings he had bought her were scattered about him on the grass, so were her bonnet and hairpins and the little beaded purse she had been clutching.

Tersely, furious with himself for not having pulled her away from the scene, Ives explained what had happened. One of the policemen took down notes, while the other helped Ives to carry Rose to the nearest seat. She opened her eyes, saw that the expression of Ives's face bent over her was as much enraged as concerned, and promptly closed them again. She moaned and murmured desolately: 'Oh, how dreadful! Oh, why did I? Please, please take me home.'

Fortunately they were not far from the park gates, and the three men between them carried her to them. Another constable arrived on the scene and gathered up the scattered treasures on the grass. Ives lifted Rose into a cab he signalled, and she who was ashamed and terrified sagged against him. 'I'm ashamed, dreadfully ashamed,' she sobbed.

'No need to be. You're a brave girl and should be proud of yourself.'

At such unexpected praise, and at the warm tone of his voice, Rose partially revived. She said: 'Oh, thank you,' and then: 'I couldn't let them kill each other.'

'They wouldn't have done that, though their impulse was to kill you for interfering. The devil of it is, that this can hardly be kept from your aunt. The police have your address and mine. I was bound to give it when they demanded it. They'll be bent on tracing those two hell-cats, and bringing a charge against them . . . requiring you – me – to give evidence.'

'I shall be disgraced for ever,' uttered Rose in consternation.

'Not so long as that, I think, especially if I . . . well, if I show that though the escapade was foolish, I am serious.'

Bemused though she was, Rose grasped his meaning, and scarcely dared to believe it. 'Are you?' she whispered, and he wondered if the innocence of her blue eyes concealed an element of calculation.

'That appears to be obligatory unless I behave as a cad,' he said dryly.

Rose was silent, though her heart was pounding. Suppose – oh suppose something truly wonderful resulted from this escapade. If so, what matter her aches and pains? They would be more than worthwhile; but she was too hazily adrift for coherent thought, and was half-asleep by the time the cab stopped at Mrs Talbot's house, and Ives lifted her out upon the pavement and rang the bell.

Thereafter all was confusion. The servants clustered round the battered Rose, while the dignified housekeeper summoned the butler, who had been in Mrs Talbot's service for years, and he sent the young footman in haste for the family doctor. Mrs Talbot, so Ives was told, was still in her drugged sleep and feeling that he could do no good here, but had better leave Rose to female ministrations, he briefly recounted what had occurred and, bidding the housekeeper tell her mistress when she awoke and was in a fit state that he would call on her as soon as she could see him, he took his departure.

The fussing maids got Rose up to her bedroom, and were followed by the housekeeper who exclaimed with horror over the scratches on her neck and cheeks. A strand of hair that had been torn from the roots was caught in the embroidery of her collar, and when her dress was removed it was seen that there was a large and angry bruise on her back at which there were fresh exclamations of dismay.

'And 'twas only yesterday we were saying that this was the dullest place; as dull as ditch-water,' cried the younger housemaid, 'and now to think of all that's happened since then. Miss Livvy's elopement, and Miss Rose set upon in the public park.'

'Where Miss had no business to be,' said the housekeeper

severely, 'and if you open your mouth so wide, Hannah, you'll swallow a fly as like as not. No word of this is to be spoken of outside the house, understand me, and if you disobey, well then I shall find out for sure, and this dull as ditch-water place won't be yours for much longer, for if there's one thing I can't abide, it's gossip about the family. You know best what your father and mother will say if you're turned out of your first place without a reference.'

Hannah flinched, for she certainly did know. Her mother would scold and scold, and her father would lay a stick across her shoulders. Mute and resentful she scurried out of the room as a bell pealed. That, said the housekeeper, would be the doctor, brought by Nathaniel, the footman. Hannah could show the way to Miss Rose's room.

CHAPTER 3

Rose was a loved member of her family, and being the eldest had been given more privileges and was considered more important than her four younger sisters. The Broughtons, much to their disappointment, had not been blessed with sons, and now Mrs Broughton was unlikely to have more children. Squire Broughton on the arrival of his first-born had not guessed that he would be so unfortunate as to father four other daughters, therefore she had been warmly welcomed, and once having formed the habit of loving her, it was not to be broken though he took considerably less interest in the girl children who followed her.

Moreover, Rose had a spirit and a lusty strength which appealed to him. It was a thousand pities she was not a boy, for she could ride well, and he had taught her how to handle both a gun and a fishing-rod. She was interested in all the details of the estate and the model farm which was his hobby, and in secret he sorrowed because the child who had once been delighted to wear breeches and thick boots, and had hugged him with joy when he had agreed that she was in need of no further schooling, had within the last year turned into what he regarded as a fine lady.

Even so he was proud of her, and would have been indignant had he guessed that in her aunt's circle her robust figure was criticized, and that even in these country parts she was considered less than a beauty. There wasn't a man he knew worthy of her, and he was impatient of his wife who, anxiously conscious that husbands must be found for five girls, hoped to marry off her eldest before Christobel, the second girl, now sixteen, left the schoolroom.

It was Rose's possible marriage that was now under discussion. He had had a thoroughly satisfactory day, rough shooting on a neighbour's estate. He had shelved his worries for a few hours, but was faced with them again in his own drawing-room where his wife awaited him, not only with tea, hot buttered toast and a variety of home-baked cakes, but with the evident determination to wring a decision from him.

'We know nothing about the fellow,' grumbled Squire Broughton, with his mouth full of plum cake.

It was bad luck from his point of view that for once in a way his wife had no visitors. As a general rule she was either out visiting or presiding over some local function; or the room was filled with ladies old and young, chirping like birds in an aviary. On these occasions he was not expected to be present. If he appeared at all, it would be to utter a few general remarks, and then to retreat to his study on the pretext of business, where a maid would bring him his tea. But this afternoon his wife had given orders that she was 'not at home' to callers. It was essential to continue the conversation which had started after breakfast that morning, and which the Squire had then said he had no time to pursue.

'Hilda, in her letter, has answered the question I put to her,' Caroline Broughton informed him, 'and although she does not say so, it is evident from what Rose has revealed that she hoped to secure him for Lavinia. Poor Hilda, she is so mortified over this elopement.'

'There's nothing she can do, m'dear, but make the best of it. Her girl is of age, and in possession of her fortune.'

'That doesn't make it easier to bear, though I dare say it is some satisfaction to her that our daughter has also behaved badly.'

'Pooh! You make too much of it. The girl was offered an afternoon's pleasure, and naturally enough accepted it.'

'But it was very wrong of her, Martin, with poor Hilda in such distress, and asleep only because the doctor had put her to sleep. It wasn't the time to think of a pleasure jaunt, and in any case she knew she would not have been allowed to go off with Mr Tresham, without anyone to chaperon her. Then as though that wasn't bad enough, to get herself mixed up in a common affray . . . it makes me shudder to think of it.'

'This fellow – what's his name? Tresham – should have taken better care of her.'

'Well – yes, but of course he did not imagine Rose would attempt to intervene in a low brawl. Most girls would have shrunk away in terror.'

The Squire chuckled. 'She's a good plucked one. Too good to be forced into marriage with a fellow we know nothing about, just because of a mild escapade.'

'But there was a piece in the paper about it, and in any case Rose is not being forced. She had a liking for Mr Tresham, who has behaved most properly in writing to ask if he can see you with a view to paying his addresses to her, though having involved her in such disgrace, let alone danger, it was the least he could do. Poor, foolish girl she has hopelessly compromised herself. All our friends are talking of it.'

'It will be nothing but a nine days' wonder, Caroline. 'Pon my word I don't understand you. You regard yourself as a tender mother, but you'd hand Rose over with your blessing to a stranger, and she only eighteen.'

Mrs Broughton gazed at her husband with resignation. When she had married him over twenty years ago, he had been a big, clumsy, sandy-haired young man with a sanguine complexion. Now at fifty he was heavier in build, and his sandy hair was greying, but otherwise there was little change in him. They had never been in love. Their marriage had been arranged by their parents. Martin Broughton had been of an age to settle down and had known Caroline all his life. Caroline had thought of marriage as her vocation. Intellectually her husband was not her equal, and she was not drawn to him physically, but she had recognized his good points and his general suitability, and was determined to make the marriage a success. That it had been, except her unfortunate failure to bear a son. His land, his ancestral home, his model farm with its dairy and prize cattle, were all objects of devotion. Since coming into his inheritance a few years ago, he had made great improvements to the estate, and had generally prospered. As for Caroline she was a power in the district, and looked up to by everyone. She ran her home with zeal and was a fond though not over-indulgent mother.

Rose, from her point of view was not an ideal daughter. Until a year ago, she had been a hoyden, and for that Caroline blamed her husband, though she understood well enough that he only encouraged Rose's forwardness because he lacked a son. At that time Rose had seemed a wonder and an object of envy to Lavinia Talbot, the delicate child who had been sent down to Derevale Manor for a country holiday. It was only when Rose changed, showed definite signs of womanliness, only when she began to take an interest in her toilet and to despair of her freckles, that Livvy had become critical and condescending, for then Rose was encroaching on her territory.

Caroline had been partly reassured by this development, though she suspected that a defiance of convention still lurked beneath the Rose who now preened herself in her flounced silks and muslins and coaxed an allowance out of her father. Her apprehensions had been justified by this really lamentable escapade, and she considered it better fortune than her daughter deserved that the eligible young man who had led her into mischief was prepared to marry her. That there was nothing but a flattered and excited readiness to accept him on Rose's part, Caroline had already discovered, and it was too bad that her husband was so unenthusiastic. If he chose, he could refuse to allow a marriage before Rose was twenty-one, and this rich American who was probably offering for her chiefly out of chivalry, could not be expected to wait for three years.

'Nobody can hand Rose over to any suitor, if she is resolutely set against it,' Caroline now pointed out, 'but she is not. I would wish to ask Mr Tresham down to stay with us, but I cannot without your consent.'

'When have I ever opposed you? You have always had your own way. A spoilt woman if ever there was one.'

The comely Caroline smiled complacently: 'Yes, my dear, you have been very good to me, though believe me I should never attempt to over-ride your definite wishes. If you dislike Mr Tresham when you meet him, then there is no more to be said, but you are always fair-minded, Martin, and I am sure if you are against him it will be for some good reason. You will not be unjust to him because you dislike parting from Rose.'

'Well, that's true,' agreed the Squire, appeased by such tactful handling, 'though you're a strange woman, Caroline. It's a puzzle to me how you can resign yourself to an American husband, who will take the girl thousands of miles away from us. More than likely we shall never see her again once he has married her.'

Caroline had no idea as yet that Ives had sold his plantation. Mrs Talbot had not mentioned it in her letter, and it was something that had gone straight out of Rose's head; not surprisingly, considering the bewildering events of the last week.

In spite of her injuries her return to Derevale Manor had been delayed by only one day. Mrs Talbot had told her firmly that she had disgraced herself and had behaved in the most heartless fashion. The police had questioned Rose, but to little avail, for Rose had said with truth that she could not remember what her assailants had looked like, except that they were horrible. They had not been traced.

Mrs Talbot was additionally indignant because it seemed as though her turbulent niece might profit by her indiscretion. Ives had called to offer apologies and to make it known that he was prepared to pay serious suit to the maltreated young creature whom he had enticed into trouble. But Mrs Talbot had received him coldly and had said that such matters were not for her. Rose's parents must deal with them.

Still shocked and bruised, with a cut lip not yet healed, and chiffon scarves drawn across her scratched face, Rose had been despatched from London by coach with Mrs Talbot's grudgingly spared housekeeper to act as duenna. Once at home she had been put to bed, her mother insisting that she stayed there, less out of solicitude, thought Rose resentfully, than as a punishment. It was some comfort to find that her father made light of her adventure. Sitting beside her bed, he had laughed uproariously as she recounted it, but it was her mother who was really important.

'Ives says he wants to marry me, if you will give me to him, Mamma,' she said. 'I saw him just before I left London, and he said he had already written to Papa.'

Caroline closely questioned her, and was feeling more or less satisfied even before her sister's letter arrived. Mrs Talbot considered it her duty to admit that Ives Tresham would be a good match for any girl, and certainly a brilliant one for Rose; but it was also her duty to point out that Ives was only paying his address out of a sense of obligation. His careless disregard of convention had brought injurious publicity on Rose, and as a gentleman he felt forced to make amends.

'It is reassuring that he has such a proper view of his responsibility,' said Caroline, 'but nothing can be decided in a hurry.' This, although she had already resolved that for nothing on earth should her tiresome daughter lose the chance of making such a marriage.

Rose's young sisters saw her as a heroine, and Christobel, two years her junior, was frankly envious. Mrs Broughton sometimes feared that there was an oddity about Christobel. She gave promise of beauty, being tall, with dark hair and large, dreamy, violet-grey eyes; and her governess declared that she was cleverer than her sister. But she was as unaccountable as Rose, though in a different way; sometimes wildly gay in a showing-off mood, which her sisters mocked; but quite as often absent-minded and distraite, given to long silences and seeking solitude.

She was in no sympathetic mood over Rose's adventure, though she had been given her share of the fairings that Rose had brought home with her. Most of these had been distributed between her sisters, though she had kept the lace handkerchief and the musical box which played God Save the Queen, and was sorry she had prevented the purchase of the pink-satin garters. Probably she could have hidden them from her mother's eyes.

'What is he like, Rose?' clamoured Elsie and Millicent, who were fifteen and thirteen respectively. Adelaide who was only ten was occupied with the tickler – flicking flies from the window.

'Handsome, tall, dark, with magnificent eyes,' boasted Rose, 'but Mamma has just told me he has been invited to stay, so you will see for yourselves. He will be here next week.'

'Will you really agree to marry him?' asked Christobel, and there was a pitying intonation in her voice which irritated Rose.

'I expect so. Why not? He is perfectly delightful, as well as being rich. Few girls would refuse him.'

'Lavinia did.'

'You're wrong, Chrissie. He hadn't asked her.'

'But you said in your letters home, before you went to the Coronation Fair, that it was a case with him, though Livvy said he was too old for her, and she thought him uncouth.'

'Goodness only knows why! Ives is barely thirty, and I think he has charming manners. But Livvy preferred her singing master who dropped a compliment with every word he uttered, and wrote verses to her, and even composed a song for her. He has long lashes and fair, curly hair – he looks quite girlish. Ives is a proper man. I admit he was taken with Livvy, but he said himself it wasn't serious enough for him to break his heart over her.'

'You will be getting him on the rebound,' said Chrissie, who had recently read a novel in which this phrase had occurred more than once.

'What if I do? If I don't, some other girl will.'

'Will you have to go to America, and live there? Oh, Rose, don't!' cried Elsie. 'It would be so melancholy without you.'

'I don't know what will happen yet, we haven't had any opportunity to discuss the future, but I think Ives intends to settle in England.'

Rose could not remember where she had picked up this information, for Ives had not told her. She knew little about him, for when they had talked it had been only about nonsensical things. Then she recalled her aunt's conversation with Sir Rodney as they drove home on Coronation day. Something had been said about Ives's intention to buy an estate in England. Rose pondered over it. She could probably coax her father into giving his consent to her marriage, more especially as she had her mother's support; but it would be easier if he knew that Ives had no intention of taking her out of England.

❋ CHAPTER 4 ❋

Two days later when Ives arrived in his own coach, which was a stylish affair with fine grey horses and a coachman and footman in dark green livery, Rose was in a state of suppressed excitement and secret anxiety that her suitor would make a good impression on her family, and they on him. She had been told that his Virginian plantation was immense, therefore Derevale would seem small, but it was set in lovely grounds with pasture land and a park beyond it, and the old house itself was tended with loving care.

Caroline Broughton, who was interested in such matters, said that it had an intriguing history, and that some remarkable people had owned it, but Rose only vaguely remembered that a past heiress of Pleasance, the old house not far away, which years and years ago had been destroyed by fire, had married a Broughton, and had brought much money into the family, thus enabling her husband to buy additional land when he inherited.

Rose supposed that her father was comfortably off, but he was not as rich as the Broughtons had been in the days of the first Georges. Her mother spoke regretfully of the licentious Henry Broughton of the Regency days, who had squandered a deal of the family fortune; but his son had been thrifty and had done his best to retrench. Rose's father, his sole offspring, had taken the same line and Caroline had helped with a fair marriage portion. Nevertheless, five daughters were a problem, and every penny the Squire could spare was already ear-marked for the dowries they would require.

The younger girls were much impressed by their first sight of Ives who was every bit as good-looking as Rose had described him. Caroline sighed with relief, for she had wondered if he could possibly be as desirable as her sister had said. The Squire was more wary, inspecting Ives, that first night at dinner, with a suspicious eye. But even he, though far from perceptive, could see that Rose was in what he called 'a twitter', and looking radiant as she gave her suitor's every word a lingering attention. Her father could not deny that the fellow had presence. His accent, though slightly harsh, was not disagreeable and even before Caroline – with Rose and Christobel – adjourned to the drawing-room leaving the two men to their wine and cigars, he had made a favourable impression on the Squire, chiefly through his genuine delight in the old house and his admiration of the country through which he had driven on his way from London.

The Squire, who realized with resignation that there would be several formalities before he gave his consent to the betrothal, wondered how he, so inept at diplomacy, could first broach the reason for Ives's visit, and was relieved when the other plunged boldly into the matter.

'I am only too conscious, sir, that being a stranger in the land I may be far from the husband you would choose for your daughter,' said Ives, 'but I hope that can be remedied. My plan is to settle in England, develop an estate, and raise a family here. In all probability I shall never again see my native land. If Rose is allowed to marry me, I shall hope to profit by your knowledge and advice, and even . . . well, I was told it might be possible for us to do business together, should you be agreeable.' He broke off as though in diffidence, fingering the stem of his wine-glass and gazing thoughtfully at its contents.

'What's on your mind?' asked the Squire bluffly.

'Pleasance,' said Ives, and raised his head to look squarely at his prospective father-in-law.

'Pleasance!' The Squire was taken aback and showed it. 'What do you know about the place?'

'Little enough, except that as a dwelling it no longer exists; though I confess that I made enquiries, and was told that the land upon which it stood is still in your possession, sir. To explain that I should say that there is a connection between my family and yours, though ours was never more than a remote cadet branch. I am distantly related to your sister's deceased husband, and far back in the archives of that family and mine, there was an Aurora Grenton whose cousin married a Tresham . . .'

'A connection by marriage only then, even at that early date,' said the Squire, but smiling, for he was not ill-pleased that this young man should show such eagerness to establish a tenuous kinship.

'That is true, but the Tresham cousin wrote an account of the house called Pleasance, though it is uncertain if she ever set eyes on it. I was told about that when only a boy, with the result that it set up what might be called a romantic longing to know more of the Grenton family.'

'The Grenton name has died out,' said the Squire. 'To tell the truth I should know less about it than I do, but that my wife has ardently searched into these old histories. The estate in the Stuart days passed to a Frenchman, whose son lived to inherit. He had but one daughter who married into the Broughton family, though before then Pleasance had been burnt to the ground. My great-great-grandmother was, I believe, a beautiful creature – you shall judge for yourself, for there is a painting of her in the picture gallery. She had a numerous family, and the marriage was a happy one, but her eldest son, my great-grandfather, was a scamp, and it took his son a lifetime to partially recover from his profligacy. Derevale is now prosperous in a modest way, though it is a grief to me and my good wife that we have no son to inherit. As of Pleasance, or what was once Pleasance, there has been no money to spare for its restoration, even had I any particular wish to restore it. The old dower house remains, though it is now a granary; but as you have taken pains to discover, the land is still mine, though it is let out for grazing. I could have sold, I dare say, but I have had no tempting offer, nor did those before me, and the rents are useful, though land is rented cheaply in these parts. What's at the back of this questioning, my boy?'

The 'my boy' indicated a tremendous change of heart, had Ives but realized it. He did not, though he was conscious of the sudden warmth in the older man's manner. He said slowly: 'When I came to England, it was with the hope of buying all that remained of the old estate, if its owner had any mind to sell. I did not then imagine I should also be entreating him – the owner – for the hand of his eldest daughter, but so by a curious train of circumstances it has come about.'

'Curious indeed,' agreed the Squire, his sluggish imagination stirred. 'Does that mean then, that if I give you Rose as a wife, you will be content to settle down here, within a few miles of us? Is that what you want – to build a new house on the foundations of one that was once the finest in the country?'

'That is what I want,' Ives said.

''Tis to be hoped then that you're well breached, for even though I give Rose the land as her marriage portion, you'll need to be if you aim to build a house worthy to vie with the old Pleasance, let alone to set out the grounds and reclaim the park which is now as wild as a forest.'

'All that I can do,' said Ives. 'My father's means were considerable, and the Virginian plantation went for a high figure, even though before selling it I gave our people their freedom. Had they gone with the plantation, as is the custom in the South where human beings are of no more account than cattle, and sometimes less, the selling price would have been higher. But I would have no such barter, though to my shame I own that my father was a trader on a big scale. It was the cause of an endless feud between us, though in his lifetime I acted as overseer and steward, partly because I was fond of the old man, partly because I knew the poor wretches would fare better if I was in charge. I did the little I could, and never knew more satisfaction as on the day I could tell each one employed in the house and on the plantation, that they were free souls, with money to keep them until they found other work.'

Ives spoke with a terse lack of eloquence, but the hand which rested on the table had clenched, and his face had darkened. The Squire voiced the popular British view when he said: 'Slavery's a thing that few of us over here can stomach, and it's been put an end to, as you know, in the Colonies. You must have had a difficult time, my boy. Your views wouldn't make you popular with your neighbours.'

'I was hated for them and called a renegade, though in the

North many are of my mind. My detestation of Southern policy served to augment the craving to establish myself in the old country, and the first thing I did was to contact Mrs Talbot, to whom my father had written, or rather he had written to her husband claiming kinship. When news of his death reached us, my father offered financial help, if necessary, to his widow; and meeting her afterwards I was astonished she was not seriously affronted. But it appears she found it touching rather than an impertinence for a remote cousin to have concerned himself with her welfare. It induced her, I think, to treat me with a special kindness.'

'If my wife is correct she wanted you for her girl,' the Squire said bluntly. 'Livvy is a beauty, though too much of a drooping lily for my taste; but it's a marvel that between them they did not hook you.'

Equally bluntly, Ives said: 'Lavinia had no fancy for me. Her heart, sir, was already engaged, and one can only hope that this fellow she has run off with is good enough for her.'

'How big a blow was it to you?' The Squire was proving that as his wife often lamented, he knew nothing of tact.

'Not a mortal one. When she feigned illness and I escorted Rose to the Coronation at the Abbey, I was already much taken with her and she showed a liking for me. The next day when I was told by Rose herself, Mrs Talbot being indisposed, of her cousin's elopement, I was, to be honest, disappointed with myself to discover how little it touched me. Lavinia's coldness and lack of interest had served as a rebuff. There was Rose though, full of life, so unspoilt that any pleasure was an excitement to her. I saw no harm in taking her along to the fair. Why on a day of general festivity leave her in that silent house, with her aunt in a drugged sleep and incapable of missing her? We had a grand time, sir. I've never known a girl of merrier spirit, or one more natural. That's what brought about the trouble; because she's natural and follows her impulses. When she saw two trollops bent on slaughtering each other, she couldn't help but try to tear them apart. But in a trice they were at her. Before I could pull her away, she was down on the grass with the pair of them on top of her.'

The Squire broke in with a laugh. 'That's Rose. You tell it well, my boy, and I'm not astonished if it was then you took a fancy to her. She's got more pluck than is good for her.'

'She has courage – more than I have,' Ives allowed, 'for when I nerved myself to call on Mrs Talbot the next day, I was shaking in my shoes. What I got from her was no more than I deserved. Being a barbarous American it hadn't occurred to me that a girl's reputation was ruined if she was taken for an outing in broad daylight, though I admit I was fit to be tied when she plunged into that mêlée. I realized I was responsible. She was knocked about before I could tear those harpies off her, and then the police were on the spot, and the termagants and their bullies, who had been egging them on vanished, and only Rose and myself there to give an account of what had happened.'

The Squire guffawed. 'Luck for you,' he said, 'that you'd already got a fancy for her. No mother with a daughter to marry would have let you get away with it.'

'Well, nobody could blame such a mother, I guess,' Ives said with a grin. 'A mettlesome piece like Rose is a responsibility.'

'You're doing the handsome thing by her, but I'd think better of it if you'd clapped your eyes on her from the first, and not on Livvy,' said the Squire, evidently hoping to provoke greater warmth.

'You forget, sir, that I met Lavinia some weeks before I met Rose, but it's my belief we'd have come together in the end without benefit of drama. It sounds fanciful I know, but there's a link. When I left Virginia, it was with the thought of Pleasance at the back of my mind. A tantalizing kind of dream. But if Lavinia had looked kindly on me, it wouldn't have brought me much nearer to what I wanted, for she's not the girl to be happy in a country life. Then along came Rose and I heard she was from this part of the world, and a daughter of the Broughton who still owned what was left of that old place. To say the least it was an odd coincidence. Rose liked me and I liked her, and once Livvy eloped and was out of my reach, then I thought I'd give fate a chance, and fate wasn't a laggard. Events were speeded up because I'd compromised Rose.'

'True enough. In the ordinary run of things you'd have

been bowing and scraping for weeks before getting down to business, and she'd have played with you as like as not, blowing first hot, then cold. She might even have refused you in the end, because the sparkle had gone out of it for her.'

'Is that her nature? Is she such a coquette?'

'I don't know, my boy. What father does know a girl's nature? A year ago, Rose was more boy than girl; muddy shoes and breeches were her style; not muslin and ribbons. But then she changed, and her mother was pleased; said it was time she grew up. I lost her though, and all I know is she's turned down several hereabouts who were after her.'

Ives thought of the waist he had spanned, the soft cheek beneath his lips, and he smiled: 'Well, I must take my chance with the rest of them. Will you drink to my good fortune, sir?'

The Squire responded promptly. 'With a heart and a half, my boy, and I'd say you have a good chance. Come to think of it, Caroline, my wife, said there'd be no cause to force the girl's consent, which shows she's in Rose's confidence. Not that I'd have had her forced, whatever the trouble she'd brought on herself, and by that I mean pretty well any trouble a wench can get herself into.'

By this time the Squire who had been drinking steadily throughout the conversation was becoming slightly maudlin, but he gazed at Ives with approval, and as the clock chimed the half-hour he got out of his high-backed chair at the head of the table, and remarked that it was more than three-quarters of an hour since his womenfolk had left them, and that his wife would be in a pretty pet if they delayed longer.

It was true that Caroline in the drawing-room had cast more than one irritated glance at the closed door, and soon with unwonted sharpness she had sent Christobel off to bed, telling Rose to stop wandering about the room; to sit down with her embroidery frame, and fix her attention on this suitable occupation.

With a resigned sigh and some sympathy for Christobel, Rose seated herself primly on the sofa. She detested embroidery, and she had been weeks over this particular specimen, constantly unpicking her faulty stitches. She knew that in the end her mother would finish it.

Then the door opened, and all Caroline's irritation passed as a cloud passes across the moon, for the Squire and Ives were plainly on such terms as she had not expected. The Squire's hand was on the younger man's shoulder, as he beamed at his wife and daughter.

'Well, now,' he drawled, slurring his words and swaying on his feet, 'we've straightened it all out, m'dear. You'll have a kind, loving son-in-law, and Rose 'ull have a kind, loving husband; what's more they'll be living only five miles away from us, and the glory of Pleasance will rise . . . will rise . . .'

'Like a Phoenix from the ashes,' supplemented Ives as the Squire searched in vain for a suitable simile.

CHAPTER 5

Ives duly proposed and was duly accepted by a demure Rose in a pale-blue muslin dress which Caroline, with the aid of a sewing maid, had fashioned for her. With its ruffled sleeves and lace-edged collar and cuffs, it was very becoming to the wearer.

'I shall do my best to make you a good wife, and I hope that in time you will learn to have a real affection for me,' said Rose, at which remark Ives looked startled.

'My dear child, I already have an affection for you,' he said, taking her hand and fondling it.

Rose felt very grown-up, and was proud of her self possession as she sat on the sofa in the drawing-room, which for this important occasion had been put at their disposal. Even a conscientious chaperon such as her mother was bound to allow her to receive a proposal of marriage without the presence of a third person.

'Well,' she said in a judicial tone, 'I imagine you do rather like me. If you had quite detested me, you would have made yourself scarce after that undignified scuffle. I cannot believe that even the most – most punctilious gentleman would have offered for a girl unless he thought there was some promise that they would have an agreeable life together.'

'I am certain we shall have a *most* agreeable life,' Ives assured her.

'Even if Livvy had not eloped, you might, when you found that Papa would give me what remains of that old Pleasance, have found it difficult to choose between us,' said Rose, 'though you could have bought the land and the ruins, I suppose, and even the treasures Papa still has, which were saved on the night of the fire so many years ago. But with all your money and hers, and everything to make life luxurious, Livvy would not have liked living in the country. Music – concerts and operas – matters more to her than anything else, even more, I dare say, than Mr Swan, and it will be to her heart's delight if she now lives in Paris.'

'Rose, cannot we stop talking about Lavinia?' asked Ives, who apart from a natural wish to forget her cousin, was loath that this hour of rare privacy should be wasted.

'Yes, if you object, though isn't it as well to get things straightened out from the beginning? I know you are not wild about me as you were about her, but it could have been only for her looks. You had no chance to get to know her, for she held you off. If you had known her you would have found that except for being musical, she is a rather silly girl. Truly I am more sensible. I had my years at being good at boy things, but I gave them up because I'm not a boy. This last year I've been learning all I could about how to manage a house; a tedious business, but I shall be able to do it quite well. I shall make a satisfactory mistress of your house, Ives.'

'I haven't a doubt of it.' Although amused, he was becoming slightly impatient. They would not be left alone for much longer. If she *must* talk, she could tell him more about Pleasance, but he did not particularly want her to talk. He turned her about and kissed her, not with haste and stealth, as when she had clung to him in the absurd, ghostly house at the Fair, but with deliberate enjoyment. He said: 'You are delicious.'

'But I'm almost plain with my freckles and my big mouth.'

'Nonsense. You are a fine girl, and I shall be proud of you. Moreover, I am convinced that we are well suited. One thing we have in common is our love of the country. You wouldn't care to live in London, would you?'

'Only for a week now and again – for a change.'

'You shall have such a change at intervals, that I promise you. Will it be exciting for you to help me to recreate that old house? Is there enough of it left for us to be able to guess what it once was like?'

'I don't know. Papa told me that to rebuild it would be your dream come true. Why didn't you tell me more when we were in London?'

'There wasn't much opportunity, and surely you would have thought my preoccupation with an old house I had only heard of as a child was fantastic, rather ridiculous.'

'Not ridiculous. To me it's romantic. Shall we drive over this afternoon and look at Pleasance? I used to enjoy playing there when I was a child; when the others were small, and still in the nursery, Chrissie and I used to coax Miss Compton, our governess, to drive over in the pony carriage with us, and we would take a picnic meal and play hide-and-seek in the spinney. You have your carriage here, and nobody would notice if we went off in it. Why don't we? Before we are prevented?'

Ives shook his head. 'Certainly not. There will be no more escapades and adventures. If we go, it will be with your Mama's consent.'

'She'd never let us go alone. She would think it most improper.'

'Doubtless. Therefore you will have to make up your mind to be proper, until we are married. Tell me, Rose, are you a little bit in love with me, or have you merely decided that marriage to me has its desirable aspects!'

'It has, of course,' said Rose, 'but if you are romantic about this old ruined Pleasance, well then, I am just as romantic about you.'

'Really? But you don't seem very excited when I kiss you and hold you – thus.'

'I daren't let myself be, because if you toss my hair and my dress about, Mama will notice it and she'll lecture me for hours about being unmaidenly. She told me I must only allow you to kiss my hand, and that you should be on your knees when you asked me to marry you.'

Ives burst out laughing. 'Is that how you want it to be?'

'No – oh, no! But you did say I had to be proper.'

'Not to the extent of sitting primly upright in my embrace – a very chaste embrace. I won't toss your pretty dress or your hair, I promise you.'

Thus encouraged Rose relaxed in his arms, and an interlude followed that was highly agreeable to them both. It occurred to Ives that the lovely, languid Lavinia would have been less stimulating than this entirely natural and honest creature; and yet at the thought of Lavinia, something within him winced. Rose had just said that he was romantic. Perhaps he was, and if he could have had Lavinia and also all that remained of Pleasance, he would scarcely have known which was the more valuable.

At the sound of a discreet cough outside the door, Rose gave a gasp and pushed him away, smoothing the bright braids of her hair as her mother came in. Ives was glad that he had given Rose her ring, had put it upon her finger immediately she had consented to become betrothed to him. Showing it to her mother, tided her over the first embarrassed moments. The cluster of diamonds and sapphires was beautiful, Caroline said, as she kissed her daughter, and then held out a gracious hand to Ives.

As he bent over the hand to kiss it, he dared not glance at Rose, for he heard a stifled giggle. In the curiously affected era of the young Victoria, which scarcely varied from that of the later Regency days, Rose was an anomaly, especially when seen in a London setting that was all elegance and polish. She was honest and innocent, and he, belonging to a younger, less mannered country could appreciate it. Doubtless a few years would temper her; she would learn something of dignity and reticence, but basically she might be always a child of nature.

'I am so pleased, so really delighted,' Caroline was saying. 'You both look happy, and you have made others happy as well. Your father, Rose, would have sorrowed had your marriage taken you far away from him. And needless to say, to know that you will be living near us is also a great comfort to me.'

Ives, straightening his tall body, glanced at Rose, who had walked over to the window and was gazing out of it. He said: 'It will take time to build our home, Madam, but I hope you and Squire Broughton will not insist on our waiting until it is ready for us.'

'By no means. My husband and I have already talked of it. This house is large enough to give you a wing for your own use until the new Pleasance is ready for you, and if you wish it to resemble the old, then I must search out various paintings and sketches I have, and show them to you.'

'Nothing will be of greater interest to me,' said Ives with truth, 'or at least, nothing except Rose herself.'

He had been conscious of a sulkily hunched shoulder, but now Rose turned back to him with her broad, radiant smile. He must be cautious not to care too much for the house which would be built under his instructions, Ives thought, or he would have to contend with a childish jealousy that would soon become boring to him.

❋ CHAPTER 6 ❋

Heavy rain the next day made it impossible to drive over to Pleasance as had been planned. Rose was vexed because she and Ives were not given the chance to be alone. Her mother and Isobel joined them on a tour of the Manor, and Christobel, plainly fascinated by Ives, was in what the family called a 'forward' mood. Rose would have tolerated that had Ives paid no attention to her, but the younger girl evidently amused him with her prattle and as he encouraged her Mrs Broughton could hardly reprove her.

'Why do you want to rebuild that horrid old Pleasance and live there?' asked Christobel. 'You will spend heaps of money on it, and then you won't like it. Why can't you both make this your home? There's the whole of the west wing, which hasn't been used since before I was born.'

'Married people, especially those of consequence, prefer to have their own establishment,' said Caroline.

'I don't believe Rose would care. She doesn't think she's of much consequence, and it would be fun to have them here.'

'We shall be here for a time,' said Rose, 'perhaps for quite a long time.'

Christobel wanted to know if the wedding would be that summer, and when Rose said it had not yet been discussed, her sister teased her to name the day.

'Why do you want to wait long, either of you? A romance of summer is much more fun than an autumn or winter one. We could have the marquee put up in the garden for the reception, and the bridesmaids' dresses would be prettier. I shall be chief bridesmaid, shall I not? That's only fair as I am next to you in age. Ives, you will have to give us all a present. Can they be jewelled bracelets? I have always wanted one with rubies.'

But that was too much for Caroline Broughton. She was shocked, and said sternly that it was a pity Christobel was now too old to be given a whipping. She would go to her room and stay there until her mother told her she could leave it.

'She meant no harm. She's only a child,' said Ives as a chastened Christobel departed.

'Not quite,' said Caroline. 'She's growing up too fast, and her governess hasn't sufficient control over her. She has shamed me by her rudeness and cupidity.'

Although Rose had been angry with Christobel, she now defended her. 'She was only showing-off. She gets over-excited and, well, I think really she's troubled and wants to brush it off with a kind of bravado. She was quite upset when she heard we should be living at Pleasance – the new Pleasance Ives plans to have built. She never did like it over there.'

'Didn't she?' Ives looked at Rose curiously. 'I thought you said you used to have happy times, and picnics in the grounds when you were children.'

'We did – and I was happy, but Chrissie had a fright there, or we thought it was a fright, didn't we, Mama?'

'We never really understood it,' said Caroline, 'and I had only Miss Compton's account of what happened. Rose was about eleven at the time, and Christobel was nine. In the summer they often drove over to the old place. On that particular day it was very hot, and both Miss Compton and Rose were drowsy after they had had their lunch. They probably fell asleep, though Miss Compton says that with her it was the lightest doze. Christobel wandered away, it seems, and presently when Miss Compton was more alert she became uneasy and went after her. There is a lake on the outskirts of Pleasance, and she found Chrissie lying on the brink with her clothes soaked and in a very odd state. She said the most peculiar things, that there had been ice on the lake; an extraordinary fancy on that hot day, and that a lady had been skating on it who had beckoned to her, invited her. She said the lady was very beautiful, and laughing, but that there was something about her which was frightening. Christobel said she didn't want to obey her, but it was as though she was pulled to her, and so she walked out upon the lake, upon the ice as she thought. But of course there was no ice, only water, and she was almost out of her depth when she heard Miss Compton calling her and managed to wade back to land, the ice and the lady having both disappeared. She must have fallen down and swooned with exhaustion, to be found by Miss Compton shortly afterwards. She was quite ill after that – some sort of fever. She had caught a chill, but even so it was an odd occurrence.'

'Not really,' said Rose. 'Chrissie had the start of a cold before we set off that day. I distinctly remember how she sniffled, and Miss Compton was half-inclined to take her home. But she thought it was nothing serious, though I suppose Chrissie must have been in a fever even then, and have been so hot she was tempted to cool herself by stepping into the shallow part of the lake. As for the rest – well, she must have either dreamt it or imagined it.'

'My dear, I am not suggesting anything else, but the incident made a strong impression on her. She still remembered it when she was well again, and since then, though it was so long ago, she has refused to go near the place by herself.'

Ives said easily: 'She'll get over it when she sees the new house being built – when it is finished. It would be too bad if she didn't, for Rose will want to have all her family visiting her as frequently as possible.'

'It's delightful to think of that,' Caroline said. 'Perhaps now, as the weather is so inclement, you would like to look through some of the old portfolios which contain papers salvaged from Pleasance when it was consumed by fire. That was in the reign of George I. All connected with the old place was collected and stored in the picture gallery here; and not long afterwards, Linnet, the daughter of the owner of Pleasance, married Laurence Broughton, whose father had recently bought Derevale Manor – this house. Linnet was a widow – her marriage had been a tragic one . . . but you can read of it for yourself.'

'Read of it? Is there an account of it then?'

'A tome,' said Rose, before her mother could answer. 'Mama has made me study it. She thought I ought to know something of my ancestors' lives – though it's the women who were interesting or near-interesting. I never have been able to get really absorbed in the old, dead past. And besides that, the handwriting is difficult . . .'

'Laurence Broughton wrote clearly,' her mother said, 'and your Papa had the manuscript bound at my request. There has always been a link between Derevale and Pleasance, and at one time the two estates were owned by members of the same family. That was in the Protectorate days. The Royalists who had owned Pleasance fled, and the Reynolds family, who were Cromwell's followers, were the most influential family in the district.'

'And then,' chimed in Rose, 'when Charles II was on the throne, Pleasance was given back to the Grentons, or rather to a French relation of Andrea Grenton's, because she was then living in Paris, and would not return, though she had married a Reynolds. It was that relation, a Count something or other . . .'

'Count Jacques Pallistier,' Caroline supplied.

'Yes, so it was. He married a French lady and brought her to Pleasance, and she . . . but Mama that really is rather odd, for she met her death skating on the lake when it was ice-covered, or at least she died soon afterwards, because she fell through and was half-drowned, and her poor babe was motherless. I had forgotten all about Chrissie's story until today. Do you think she could have had a vision of Eloise Pallistier?'

'It is unlikely. I should think anything so absurd,' said her mother repressively. 'Christobel, as we are agreed, had a fever and dreamt or imagined it all.'

'What happened in later years?' asked Ives.

Rose looked blank. She said: 'I cannot remember much of it, but the baby boy grew up and became an architect, and he was Linnet's father.'

'Her first husband was a very bad man,' said Caroline, 'very cruel to her. He became a Jacobite and was executed in the reign of the first George. It was soon afterwards that Pleasance was struck by lightning in a great storm, and was burnt almost to the ground. Part of the stone walls are all that remain of the old building. Linnet's second marriage was a happy one. They had five or six children, but the eldest son was – regrettable, as I dare say my husband has told you. He has suffered much through that ancestor's sins. This is a colourless record, my dear Ives, but you may find the written one more interesting than this idle girl of mine would lead you to believe.'

Rose only pretended to pout. She knew her mother was well pleased with her, for was she not most suitably betrothed? She had never been more than passable at her lessons, but what did that matter now? Ives did not expect her or require her to be clever. However, it would be wise, since he was obviously fascinated by the family history, to profess a reasonable interest in it.

She said: 'There are the pictures which were saved from the fire, but there's nothing of great value, is there, Mama – not now? Papa's grandfather sold everything.'

'He did indeed,' Caroline sighed. 'Once there were some exquisite French chairs and tables, and a gold dinner-service which Linnet inherited, and which became the pride of Derevale. It must have been worth a fortune. The old portraits are not particularly good paintings, or they would surely have gone with the rest.'

Ives was no expert and he could not have said if the paintings had much artistic value. They were not the work of any famous painter, but as likenesses he was instantly convinced they were of interest.

'What a remarkable resemblance to Rose,' he said, standing beneath the canvas of a plump, fair young woman in the square-necked, tight-bodiced dress of the Tudor period. Though it had been painted so many years ago, there was still more than a hint of bright colouring in the cheeks and the ruddy hair.

'That was the first Grenton of any importance,' said Rose. 'She had a rather odd name – Annis. There was no male heir, so she inherited Pleasance from her father. She was a lady-in-waiting, or something of the kind, to Queen Jane Seymour. You see, Mama, I have had more industry than you supposed, for I know a good deal about ancestress Annis.'

'Only I fear,' said Caroline, 'because you were told so many times that you resembled her, and became curious about her.'

'Strange that a likeness should be perpetuated through several generations,' said Ives, much struck, and loath to tear himself away from the contemplation of the picture, until Rose said that Linnet Broughton was something of the same type, though much prettier. Her portrait was at the other end of the gallery.

Linnet, Ives agreed, had evidently been a beauty, and she had tender eyes and a sweet mouth. But it was the compelling forcefulness of the pictured Annis Grenton that fascinated him. The portrait of her husband who had been a great scholar, so Caroline told him, and had written a history which in its day had made him famous, seemed pale and lifeless in comparison; so did that of her son, who had run away from home to become an actor. He was particularly interested, however, in the Aurora who, half-French, had married into the Grenton family, and with her husband had lived most of her life in Paris. The paintings of her famous daughter Andrea, who had provided the first link with Derevale by marrying a Reynolds, were still well known, and he wondered that none of them were to be seen here.

'We do have some of her sketches,' said Caroline, and

took from a cupboard an armful of portfolios and books, of which burden Ives hastened to relieve her. 'It's certainly a great pity she did not paint a portrait of her great-aunt Lucilla, with whom she lived for many years, and who died just before Andrea escaped from England, and Cromwell's men took possession of Pleasance.'

'She must have been about the nicest of the Grentons,' said Rose, as Ives turned over the old drawings, most of them sketched on vellum. 'It was vastly romantic to escape from England dressed as a boy, with her lover who was wounded disguised as an old woman, and riding pillion.'

'She was a very clever artist,' said Ives, not so much impressed by the sketches of the fragile, elderly woman who had been Lucilla Grenton, as by the background drawings of the old house. Stately, beautiful, and mainly early Tudor, Andrea Grenton's pencil had endowed Pleasance with a fairy-like unreality.

'Shall we settle on Gothic?' he asked Rose.

'For the rebuilt Pleasance? Well, I suppose, yes . . . if that's the style you admire. The drawings make the old house look almost a castle.'

She was not enthusiastic, and would have much preferred a plainer mansion of flat, Georgian lines, but Ives who might have given way to any whim of Lavinia's was not disposed to take Rose's whims seriously. She was, after all, but an untutored, country girl, and in years scarcely more than a child. Only a Pleasance as much a replica as possible of the old building would satisfy Ives.

Rose's mother, realizing what an immensely expensive undertaking this would be, was more impressed than her daughter. Rose would be reigning as mistress over an establishment of far more grandeur than any other in the country.

✻ CHAPTER 7 ✻

Later, when the old estate was explored, it was impossible for Rose to keep pace with Ives's enthusiasm. As a child the grounds had enchanted her because they were half-wild and thus exciting for games of the more adventurous kind. Once, she had been severely reprimanded for climbing almost to the summit of a tall tree, and in a pet she had hidden herself in the spinney, where the bushes were dens, while Miss Compton searched for her and called to her that it was time to return to Derevale.

But today the deserted gardens seemed dark and uninviting. Although the rain had passed over, the sunshine was fitful. It was a year or more since Rose had been near Pleasance, and she was now keenly aware of the prevailing desolation. Only the shell of the old house remained; stone walls and gaping apertures where there had once been windows. A profusion of ivy and other creeping plants encircled them. As for the terrace, that was now a mass of weeds.

The acres beyond the gardens were in an orderly condition, for they had been maintained by the farmers who rented them, but the park, as the Squire had said, was as wild as a forest.

'Can it really be brought into order again?' asked Caroline Broughton with some misgiving.

Pleasance, itself, had never been of much concern to her, though she had been interested in the family history, interwoven as it was between those who had lived at Pleasance and those who had occupied Derevale Manor.

More than once she had urged her husband to sell the land for what it would fetch, and could not understand why he had resisted her, for in the early days of marriage they had needed money for the repairs necessary at Derevale. She could only suppose he had a sentimental affection for the old ruin. Now she was glad of it. Ives had refused to accept the land as Rose's dowry; had insisted on paying an extravagant price for it. He would, he said, gladly dispense with a dower but if the Squire for pride's sake persisted, he would appreciate it if Rose brought with her all that still remained of the treasures salvaged from the fire at Pleasance.

Little enough that was, thought Caroline; a few pictures that might be worthless, a quantity of manuscripts, some personal trifles that could not be of much value or the Squire's spendthrift grandfather would certainly have disposed of them. Even had Pleasance been as well preserved as Derevale Manor, Caroline would not have cared to live there, but a new, grand, modern house would be a wonderful home for Rose.

As Caroline gazed around her she had the unpleasant feeling that in these last years the trees had moved nearer to the house; and in a sense they had, for having received no attention for a lifetime, they were now spreading in all directions. If there had been a house still standing, they would have darkened all the front rooms. Rose startled her by saying, almost as though she had read her thoughts: 'It's as though they have taken possession. As though human beings are intruders here.'

'Nature always takes possession, when there is long neglect,' said Caroline and asked Ives, who had walked through the space that had once been the main entrance, if he would have all that remained of the old Pleasance pulled down.

'I shall have to find an enthusiastic architect,' replied Ives, 'and take his advice. So far as I can tell the walls are sound and so are the foundations. Possibly they can be incorporated in the new building, but they must be well tested. I did hear, indirectly, of an architect – one Owen Allen by name, who lives at Lincoln, and has done good work there. Lincoln, judging by the map, is not too far from here, and my thought was to engage all his time, until the new Pleasance is completed. I have written to him to that effect. Whether this is possible depends on his commitments, but I am prepared to pay twice the sum he would normally command in the course of a year.'

Rose gazed at him with her mouth open, and her mother too was sufficiently startled to refrain from reproving her when she said: 'Ives, if you can even think of doing that you must be vastly rich.'

'Well – yes – perhaps I am by English standards,' he admitted.

'But *how* rich?' Rose persisted.

'Do you expect me to produce figures here and now, child? Rest assured that I have satisfied your father.'

Recovering herself, Caroline said: 'Rose, it is exceedingly ill-bred to discuss money affairs.'

'Why is it?'

'Such matters are not the concern of females, and should not engage their thoughts.'

'But Mama, is that not rather silly?' Rose protested. 'When I am mistress of my own household I shall be expected to keep accounts and not to incur debts, unless Ives is so rich that extravagance will be of no importance to him.' Caroline said, 'Extravagance is always sinful, even in the most affluent households. It is said that our young Queen has been carefully instructed in ways of economy.'

'It would be foolish to squander a large fortune,' agreed Rose, 'but a wife should know how lavish she is expected to be. I shall enjoy being rich, but if Ives were poor I should still want to marry him. I am in love, and I desire him for myself, quite apart from what he can give me in the way of servants and clothes and jewels.'

Caroline was genuinely confounded, for the gaze her daughter turned upon her betrothed was ardent and intense. More than that – Caroline sought in her mind for the right word, and decided that it was a hungry gaze, and for a girl to speak so, avowing her love and desire, would have been thought by some to be actually improper. Even to Caroline, who was aware of Rose's innocence, it was unpleasant.

'Do not speak in that outrageous fashion,' she said sharply, though aware that Ives was with difficulty suppressing his mirth. 'To be desirous is natural for a husband, but not for a wife. Her part is to be obedient, submissive. As for love – before marriage you can have no knowledge of it. Naturally you have a regard for your future husband, and a great respect for him – but that is all.'

'Respect is what a girl gives to her parents,' said Rose mutinously.

'She certainly should do so; not that your respect has ever

been conspicuous. In that way you have been a disappointment and anxiety to me, and I only hope that when Ives is your husband he will have cause to be more satisfied with you.'

'Mama, if you talk in such a way, he will be afraid to marry me.'

'Not so.' Ives who divined that Caroline was now seriously disturbed, spoke with pacifying indulgence. 'Dear Mrs Broughton, it may be that I am less exigent than the average Englishman, but I should be very disappointed if Rose did not already love me. Respect is a dull word and a dull attitude.'

'It is essential,' said Caroline firmly.

'But,' pleaded Rose, 'it's fun to be in love, and I was, from the beginning, even on that first day at the Coronation service. Of course I imagined then that Ives would marry Livvy. I did not dream she would disobey Aunt Hilda, and I had no idea what she was planning with Mr Swan, but I thought – I thought – '

'What did you think?' asked Ives.

'Oh, nothing really . . . except that Livvy was fortunate.' Rose's long lashes came down to veil her too candid eyes. 'When I say I was in love – well, I have heard that many women were with Lord Byron, though they never met him – there was no harm in that, was there?'

'Possibly not,' said Caroline, 'but it was extremely foolish, and Lord Byron, though I would not deny his greatness as a poet, was an unworthy object.' Suddenly, unaccountably weary, she wished herself at home, not in this angled garden with the ruin of the old house towering above her. She said: 'It is time we returned.'

'Oh, Mama, no!' Rose was dismayed. 'Ives has not seen half of it. He said he wanted to walk through the grounds and down to the lake.'

'Walking through the grounds in the state they are in would be difficult, and certainly destructive to your gown, my child.'

'Ives will clear a path for me, and this dress is only one of my old cottons. I put it on especially, remembering the briars. It is of little consequence what happens to it.'

'Will you not trust Rose to me for half an hour, while you rest in the carriage?' Ives persuaded.

Caroline wavered, torn between her desire to oblige him, and her duty as a chaperon. She told herself that she could hardly expect Ives to conform to English notions of propriety, which he evidently thought absurd. He was no profligate, he was formally pledged to Rose, and it would be embarrassing to her as well as to the two young people if she insisted that Rose must sit in the carriage with her while he explored the grounds alone.

'It is not that I do not trust you, but that it is not the custom,' she said weakly. 'But if you will promise to be away no longer than half an hour . . . it will take you fully as long to get to the lake and back . . .'

'I will time it by my watch,' Ives said, 'and then you will know there has been no dalliance.'

Caroline gave way. She felt completely exhausted, which was extraordinary, as she had really done nothing to cause fatigue. It was not unusual for Rose to be argumentative and obstinate, but hitherto she had always been able to assert her authority. She liked Ives, and although he came from what to Caroline was an only half-civilized country, she had no complaint to find with his courtesy; but nevertheless he was leagued with Rose against her. Settled in the carriage and pleased that the coachman had turned the horses at the top of the drive so that they were facing away from the ruin, the sense of overwhelming fatigue passed but not her uneasiness.

Rose was a headstrong, wilful girl, she thought, and it was fortunate that she would soon be under a husband's control. There had been something unpleasant in her open possessiveness; something shameless, and hero-worship though it might be, it was unheard of to admit that she had been in love with Ives before he had shown the least interest in her.

Was Rose less ingenuous than she seemed? All she had said today might be construed as the proof of clumsy innocence. It was fanciful to suspect anything else, Caroline admitted, but there was an oppressiveness about this deserted place which evoked apprehension. Much had happened through the years beneath the roof of the now roofless house. Though glossed over, there had been dark pages in its history. She glanced at the small gold watch pinned to the front of her bodice and sighed, for Ives and Rose had been gone for only ten minutes. She should not have allowed this unaccompanied exploration. She doubted if any of her friends who had grown-up daughters would have been so reckless; and there was really no excuse. She could have brought Christobel with them to make a third, ignoring her second daughter's tiresome aversion to Pleasance.

At that point, Caroline's thoughts became hazy. She dropped back into her corner of the carriage and closed her eyes, drifting into a light doze.

❋ CHAPTER 8 ❋

'We shall never do it in half an hour, though if we don't Mama will be annoyed. Shall we turn back?'

Rose looked ruefully at the long scratch on her arm for although, in what had once been a delightful rose garden, Ives had held back thorny branches from bushes that had long since produced nothing but wild blooms, one had eluded his grasp and tearing at her sleeve the thorns had caught at the flesh beneath.

'As you wish,' said Ives. 'We can always come here another day and start with the lake.'

'I shan't be allowed. I've already shocked and annoyed poor Mama. It's impossible to be honest with her. Impossible with anyone I dare say.'

'Not with me. I shall never be shocked whatever you say.'

Rose flung him a laughing, coquettish glance. 'Don't tempt me. You easily could, and then I might startle you. Suppose I were to tell you that after that horrid fight in the Park, when we were driving home, I knew you would think it only right to offer for me, and although you were in love with Livvy I decided I would accept you.'

'That doesn't surprise me in the least. You would not have gone with me that day or allowed me to kiss you had you not liked me and decided to profit by Lavinia's elopement.'

'It was quite disgraceful of me. Mama evidently thought

it disgraceful to have fallen in love before you did, and it *was* extraordinary, don't you think?'

'Why should I think it extraordinary?'

Rose stared at him, and then she laughed. 'You are very conceited, Mr Tresham.'

'And you, Miss Broughton, are a designing minx.'

'I know I am. I did not, of course, intend to be involved in that disgusting brawl, but I had been turning over in my mind how I could ensnare you. You had shown that you were interested in this old place; and you were interested in me because it belonged to my father. Do you remember how we talked about it in whispers that first evening we met, while Livvy played the piano, and Aunt Hilda frowned at us? I knew from what Livvy had said that she would hold out against taking you, though I thought she might give way in the end, unless you tired of her and turned to someone else, and I wondered how I could contrive to get you here, to see what was left of Pleasance. I thought I might invent a story – that Papa was hard-pressed for money and would be glad to sell, and then you would come down here to inspect.'

'Rose, our conversation was trivial. You could not have known I should be interested as a purchaser.'

'But I did. It was an instinct or an intuition, but I did not suppose I would win so easily. I thought it would be a battle between Livvy and me.'

'How could it be when Lavinia had made all the arrangements to elope with Swan?'

'Well, I didn't know that, but I still feel that she and I . . . that we have not finished with each other.'

Rose shivered as they emerged from the tangle of the rose garden, and Ives said: 'She has written to you to say how happy she is, and that Paris is so wonderful she will never want to return to England.'

'Yes, I know, but . . . oh, don't let's talk about her. We can get back to the drive by way of what was once a tennis court. I can't plunge again through that rose wilderness.'

'Very well then, my dear, but you must lead the way as I am a stranger here.'

'And yet when the papers are drawn up it will all be yours. It must seem fascinating to you.'

'It does. Don't race on at such a rate. As we have given up our project to walk to the lake, we can afford to spare a few minutes. Let me look at that scratch on your arm. Is it painful?'

'It stings – but not badly.'

Ives rolled up the torn sleeve. 'I never saw a prettier arm, nor a more delightfully dimpled elbow. My sweet Rose, your skin is as smooth as cream.'

'Do you really admire my looks?' she asked doubtfully. 'Nobody thought much of them in London. I showed up badly beside Lavinia.'

'You are an entirely different type, but just as enchanting in your way. Kiss me.'

'Oh, Ives, I know I shouldn't. All the books say not.'

'What books?'

'Those about etiquette and how a girl should behave, especially when she is betrothed and it is so necessary she should be reverenced by her future husband.'

'Do you want me to reverence you? Be honest now.'

'I don't know – how can I know?'

'Rose, you said, much to the scandalization of your Mama, that you loved me and desired me . . . did you mean it?'

'Yes, and it was shocking of me. Poor Mama only survived because she was sure I didn't know what I was saying. Oh, Ives . . .'

Her lips were his, and so for a few minutes was her rounded body, at least to the extent of permitting him to fondle her, or as much as could be discovered of her beneath a whale-boned bodice and a froth of petticoats.

'Women must be half-fainting on a warm day,' said Ives.

'Muslins are very thin. Oh, Ives, I'm glad we shan't have to be engaged for very long.'

'I should run away with you as Swan did with Livvy.' But even as he lightly uttered her cousin's name, an unexpected wave of envy broke over him as he thought of Swan's marital rights. He guessed that there would be an allure about Lavinia of which the uncomplicated Rose knew nothing. He could picture her; slender, silent, passive but sensuously acquiescent, and in all probability Swan, that limply handsome young man, was a poor lover.

But how fruitless it was to dwell on Lavinia! He had Rose who amused him, of whom he was every day becoming fonder – also he had Pleasance, his new Pleasance, or would have it within the space of a year or so. It could scarcely be finished so soon, but there would be a few rooms ready for occupation.

'I wish we hadn't to live at Derevale for months, perhaps even longer,' said Rose, as she led the way by a less overgrown route to the broken-down hedge through which they could scramble and thus emerge upon the drive.

'But it's most generous of your parents to offer the west wing to us as a temporary home; and as they say we shall be private and separate there.'

'So they think – they mean it of course, but I know my young sisters. They'll never leave us alone, and at their ages how can we make them understand that they won't be always welcome?'

Ives said: 'I shall endeavour to implant this in their minds, without offending their tender susceptibilities.'

'Well, but there is the Dower House,' suggested Rose, and Ives stared at her uncomprehendingly.

'You can see the roof through those trees.' Rose pointed a finger. 'There isn't time to look at it now. I suspect Mama has her eyes fixed on her watch, but you can go over it by yourself anytime. It has been used as a granary, but you could clear all that out, and if you bought new furniture, it would soon be made comfortable.'

'Are you sure? If it has received no care, the place may be tumbling to pieces.'

'But it *has* received care. If it was tumbling down it would be no good as a granary. It's years since I've been inside, but it was a pretty house with an arch in the drawing-room, held up by pillars, and mullion windows. It would be quite big enough. There must be a dozen rooms. Of course it will need to be redecorated, but if the men were paid well enough, they would have it ready by the end of the summer. You can,' said Rose as an afterthought, 'see the old ruined walls of Pleasance from the top windows.'

'That's a wonderful suggestion. As I knew the house existed, I only wonder I did not think of it myself.'

'How could you, when you had never seen it? For all you knew it could be no better than a barn or stables, but I know it's exactly the same as before the fire that was the end of Pleasance . . . or at least what seemed the end until you came along.'

'I'll give myself the pleasure of looking over it tomorrow,' said Ives, 'though we can hardly drag your poor Mama out here again. Today's expedition has sufficiently fatigued her.'

'It can't be just that. She's always active, always in demand, but perhaps I tire her, and it's a heavy kind of day. But examine it for yourself. If you ride over with a groom, he will show you the way, and find out who has the key. Then you can make up your mind.'

Ives's mind was already made up. The Dower House, if it was made fit to live in, was where he and Rose would spend the first year of their married life, and perhaps longer. His pleasure as he contemplated this dispelled the image of Lavinia. No more than Rose had he relished living indefinitely at Derevale Manor, but there had seemed to be no help for it, and it was the natural solution as he would want to be near Pleasance while it was being rebuilt. But at the Dower House he would be within sight of his gradually forming creation. He would be enabled to overlook every stage of the work, and when at last the towers, the gables and the shining walls rose above the trees, he would see them from the windows of his temporary home. With that thought in mind he experienced an accession of affection for Rose, and he pressed her arm against his side. She would be the right wife for him. Hadn't he always known it? Otherwise, would the fact that he had compromised her have induced him to offer for her? He doubted it. There had been no compulsion put upon him. The reverse in fact, for although Mrs Broughton might be anxious to see Rose married, the Squire was reluctant.

Pleasance would need a mistress, and who could be more suitable than one in whom there ran the blood of the Grentons? Much diluted it was true, only a thin, small thread of it, but the connection was still there, and when they were married and Rose bore him a son, the old name could be revived. Idly his mind collected those which had been familiar in the days of the Tudors and the Stuarts, when the old Pleasance must have been at the zenith of its glory.

Nicholas, Jeremy, Rupert. Any of them would sound well with Grenton-Tresham appended to them.

'You're dreaming about it all, and have shut me out,' Rose accused.

'Far from it.' He looked down at her with a smile so tender that it was as though her heart turned over. 'Truly I was in a dream, but you, my love, were in the centre of it.'

Far more often that he guessed, Rose was conscious of her inadequacy; but not at that moment for she believed him. Old ruin, or new magnificent mansion, Livvy would not have cared for Pleasance, because it was in the depths of the country and she would be separated from the world of music. But she – Rose – would love Pleasance because it was precious to Ives.

Caroline Broughton aroused from her doze as they approached the carriage, and she smiled to see them walking as lovers, hands linked, and Ives's head downbent as Rose smiled up at him.

CHAPTER 9

'It's wonderful how warm and cosy this old house is, but when it was first built, years and years ago, I suppose whoever designed it had some elderly person in mind – because it was to be a dower house I mean; the one in which the lonely, ageing widow retreated.'

Rose laughed cheerfully as she spoke, finding it quite impossible to vision a day when she would be a dowager.

'It's the thickness of the walls,' said Christobel, 'and the new windows that Ives has had fitted to replace the rattling old ones. They keep out draughts. Then, too, the rooms are not over-large, and it's a good idea in winter to have velvet *portières* over the doors.'

'What practical explanations, but you're right of course.

I wonder if the dowagers hated to be turned out of the magnificent Pleasance.'

Christobel said, knitting her brow in thought: 'I don't believe this house was ever occupied by dowagers. I've been reading the family history, and there's no mention of it. I know you couldn't be bothered to read it properly, but it's immensely interesting. In the autumn when I had that bad cold which clung for such a long time, Mama suggested I should study these papers, and she borrowed them from Ives. I thought it would be boring and tiresome making out all the different handwriting, but after a while it became so fascinating that I didn't mind. Someone in every generation of the Grenton family kept a desultory kind of journal, though sometimes they only wrote of important events. I don't wonder that Mama spent so much of her spare time assembling all the papers, and she even wrote notes on slips as a kind of guide to link the years. Laurence Broughton, the last to keep a connected journal, had the same idea, though he wrote a kind of résumé of his wife's family. It seems as though the Broughtons were not sufficiently interesting. He writes that he came of a healthy, undistinguished stock, who seem to have had a gift for a happy, family life, and that ordinary happiness though most desirable, is not the material which makes an absorbing journal.'

'How pleased Mama must have been to see you caught up in what was her hobby for years,' said Rose. 'I was a disappointment to her. Those old journals kept me yawning till the tears came into my eyes. As for Ives, he has skimmed through some of them, but he has had no time to read them thoroughly, and I'm glad of it, or I might not have got a word out of him for hours on end.'

'I quite enjoyed the last stages of my cold,' Christobel said. 'It was comfortable in bed with lots of pillows and a fire and one of the big oil-lamps instead of a candle. Mama wouldn't let the others bother me, because Dr Sysop said I must rest my throat and not talk, and I had blackcurrant tea to drink which I love . . . what a strange lot they were, those Grentons who lived at Pleasance.'

'Were they? They don't seem to have done anything in

particular, except Andrea Grenton who married a Reynolds who was a Royalist, though all his family were Roundheads. It must have been a terrific adventure when she escaped from England with him, and afterwards she became famous as a painter. The only Grenton who ever was.'

'Andrea must have been a dear person,' said Christobel thoughtfully, and with a smile that was oddly tender as though she had personally known and loved the Civil War heroine, 'but there was nothing mysterious about her. All her life was lived in the open. She had no frightening secrets.'

Rose looked at her sister curiously, aware that she had a more introspective mind than her own; that she was clever, imaginative and unusual. She was also ripening into beauty – a dark-haired maiden with eyes as blue as her father's, as blue as Rose's, but larger and more expressive, and fringed with long black lashes that curled upwards. She was considered rather delicate, and at present was certainly too thin, but she was not hoydenish as Rose had been at her age. Even her mother who rarely praised, commended her grace.

'But *had* any of the others secrets, or are you only imagining they had?' Rose asked.

'It may be partly imagination,' conceded Christobel, 'but not wholly. Some of those who wrote about Annis Grenton were conscious of them – Lucilla, her granddaughter for instance, though one only hears of her through Andrea's journal. And there was the Patience Reynolds who was Jacques Pallistier's second wife and brought up his son by his first French wife. Laurence Broughton records his own as well as his wife's impressions of Patience when she was dying . . . she had a heavy weight on her mind, poor thing . . .'

'I remember when I was forced to read about the family, that it was the women who seemed more interesting,' said Rose. 'When you come to think about it, it often is the wives, for they have to plan things and be secretly clever to get their own way, while the husbands give their orders, which are not always carried out exactly as they suppose. That isn't the case between Ives and me. As long as I approve of all he is doing about Pleasance, I can behave much as I choose, certainly about money, for he is the most generous of husbands.'

'That's not difficult for him. He has so much.'

If there was a slight disparagement in this remark, Rose did not discern it, for she said complacently: 'Yes, indeed. He's the richest landowner in the county. I little thought that people who live hereabouts would ever treat me as a lady of importance, but they do, you know. Isn't it absurd?'

Although she laughed merrily, she would have been displeased had Christobel agreed with her, but the younger girl only said: 'It's unusual to be important at nineteen, unless one is born of a great family, and the Broughtons were never great.'

'But there's the Grenton strain. You say they were unusual, and people say I am very like the picture of Annis Grenton.'

'I don't think you are, Rose – not really. It's only that you are fair and plump, and so was she. Your features are quite different. You are more like great grandmother Linnet, and she, though beautiful, seems to have had a simple sort of nature. It must have been terrible for her when she was married to Neil Haviland, who was a wicked roué, though a brave man. She loved him too. Think how frightful to be married to a man hanged at Tyburn.'

'But that was because he was a Jacobite, and some Jacobeans were noble.'

'Not that wretch who deserted Linnet and squandered her fortune and made her wretched. She must have felt she had come to the end of everything when she was sent down to Pleasance to live with her step-grandmother, in order to get over it. Neil Haviland surprised her there you know, and demanded sanctuary as a rebel, which I suspect Linnet would have given him, only that her mother who was staying at Pleasance would have none of it. She must have realized that if he died Linnet would be free to start her life all over again, and she gave him up to the Militia who were out hunting for him.'

'They were certainly stirring times, Chrissie. We're dull enough nowadays in comparison, but very comfortably dull.'

Rose yawned and shifted restlessly in the big chair where she was sitting, occupied with the making of a small garment in white silk and lace. In the April of 1837 and seven months' married, she was expecting her child before the end of July, and it would have been thought very odd and unnatural if she had not wished to make some of the garments for her baby's layette. But she was no better at needlework than in the past, and had little doubt but that her mother would finally take the small garment and complete it.

Christobel said: 'I can't imagine a comfortable dullness in connection with Pleasance. For all its beauty it has always been a sinister kind of house.'

'But there will be nothing sinister about the new Pleasance. Ives and Owen are enthusiastic about it, and it certainly sounds as though it will be wonderful by the time it is finished; which won't be for another year at least. Ives says they can afford to be more leisurely because we are so comfortable here for the time being, and what did happen there to make it sinister except for Neil Haviland being given up to justice?'

'Many things I'm sure, though they are not clear. Andrea hints at some wickedness for which Annis Grenton was responsible. Her granddaughter found out about it. But there are pages missing in the journal, perhaps they were deliberately destroyed, and then there was Patience whom Linnet loved. Laurence as well as Linnet was with her when she died as a very old woman, and she confessed that she was at least partly responsible for the death of Jacques's first wife, who went skating when she was near to having her baby. Patience could have prevented her, she *should* have prevented her. Eloise was in a frail state though reckless, and should have been treated as an invalid; but Patience let her go, knowing it might mean her death, hoping that it would . . . and die she did.'

Rose shivered slightly, saying: 'It's uncanny, when one remembers that odd experience of yours. Even if it were no more than a feverish dream, why should you have had such a dream?'

'It was more than a dream, Rose. One forgets dreams and they are nearly always confused, but I remember distinctly every detail; thinking I saw ice on the lake instead of water, and that beckoning woman, wearing such clothes as are not worn nowadays. She was beautiful, and she laughed and tempted me. I wouldn't live at Pleasance for the world. Even the house is too near for my comfort.'

'But nobody will be living at Pleasance – *that* Pleasance,' said Rose, with the obtuseness she could sometimes show.

'The foundations are the same and the grounds. When I am walking in them I often feel – not comfortable.'

'Oh, Chrissie, you are too fanciful! They will be quite different according to the landscape plan I have seen. Ives is having the rose garden set farther away from the house, and what was once a yew garden will be greatly enlarged. The terrace will remain of course, though there must be new marble steps.'

'I wonder if the alteration will be resented,' said Christobel dreamily.

'I shall get really cross with you in a minute, Chrissie. I never heard such nonsense.'

'In a way it's nonsense,' Christobel agreed, 'but to me everything around here seems to have its own individual life. Laurence Broughton describes it well when he writes about the last few days before Pleasance was destroyed. It was most extraordinary weather; weeks without rain: hot, airless, sunless, and they all saw beings that were not really there – as though it were too hot for the old shades to sleep. Perhaps they knew there would be a storm which would wreck the home where they had been able to dwell undisturbed. There *is* something strange about this place, Rose. We have nothing like it at Derevale, though it's equally old. I'm not the only one to be conscious of it – Owen is too. He says that when he's alone, inspecting the day's work after the men have left, he often turns round thinking someone has approached soundlessly and is at his elbow; but there's never anyone.'

The mention of Owen Allen, the young architect engaged by Ives, diverted Rose's thoughts from Christobel's fantasies. She said: 'If Mama knew how much you were seeing of Owen, she would take alarm.'

'I dare say. Mama expects us all to make marriages as satisfactory, in a worldly way, as yours is.'

'It's satisfactory in every way. I adore Ives, and the baby will make everything even more wonderful. But Chrissie, you can't be thinking of Owen as a husband. It would never be allowed.'

'Why not? He's young, clever, good-looking and kind. What more could he be?'

'He could be rich; he could be of good family. He's certainly not a person of fortune – and we don't know anything about his people. At least I don't. He may have told you about them.'

'Not very much. Owen is one of a large family, and they live in Lincoln. He has two sisters. One is married to a doctor; the other is a kind of nun.'

'Good gracious! Why? Are they Catholics? Is she terribly ugly or something?'

'It's an Anglican order, and she is the head of it. Some years ago they started a home for orphan girls. I believe Owen's sister is very handsome. People do have vocations, you know.'

'Yes, but I always thought they were plain girls or spinsters who couldn't get a husband. What was Owen's father? Has he any brothers?'

'His father,' said Christobel, 'owned a printing business, but he has retired and Owen's brothers – he has four – carry it on. Two are married, the other two are not. Owen's parents are quite old, for he is the youngest. He was, he says, an afterthought. He always had a gift for drawing, and he was articled to an architectural firm when he was only a boy. Then his father set him up on his own account. Owen has worked hard and has made quite a name locally. Ives met someone in London for whom he had designed a country house, and they could not say enough in his praise. That is why Ives engaged him to design the new Pleasance and so superintend the building of it.'

'That's all very creditable,' said Rose, 'but it would be ridiculous to become serious about him.'

'Why? I've heard you say you would have married Ives had he been poor.'

'It was easy for me to say it, and I should have wanted to, but I wouldn't have been allowed. Neither will you be allowed to marry Owen. For one thing you are only just seventeen – too young to know your own mind, and Owen is no more than twenty-seven or -eight with his way to make. It's hopeless.'

'Nothing is hopeless if one cares enough. I love Owen and he loves me. We – we feel that we were made for each other.

Nothing can keep us apart for ever. I mean it, Rose.'

Her elder sister gazed at her with dismay. Christobel had always been determined, even as a child. For all her delicate appearance there was steel in her nature. When their parents came to hear of this there would be trouble, thought Rose.

'Oh, I blame myself,' she said, 'for making it easy for you to see so much of each other, but you seemed too young to be thinking of marriage, and agreeable though Owen is, he's not exactly our class. How could he have so presumed?'

Christobel laughed with a tinge of mockery. 'We're not aristocrats – at least the Broughtons weren't, and as for the Grentons, Linnet's father was an architect. Owen will, I believe, be famous one day, as famous as Sir Christopher Wren. I know I'm young, but many girls have married at seventeen – not that I'm thinking of an immediate marriage.'

'I should hope not.'

'I know as well as you, Rose, that it wouldn't be allowed. If necessary Owen and I can wait for four years until I am of age. It might be even better for him if we did. I should grieve to be a drag on him.'

'It isn't so easy to wait,' said Rose, remembering her own passionate impulses at the time of her engagement.

'Perhaps for you it was difficult. It won't be so hard for Owen or for me. Our minds, our thoughts are in unison.'

'Well, but . . .' Rose broke off. She had been about to say that it was so also with herself and Ives, but that would have been untrue. The spiritual quality which Christobel described had had no part in Ives's attraction for her. It was aggravating to have her sister putting her own love affair upon a lofty pedestal, but Rose suppressed her irritation. 'I shall tell nobody about it,' she said, 'though I pray you will conduct yourself with discretion.'

'Oh, we shall!' Christobel laughed as though Rose had said something amusing. She would scarcely have confided in her had she not felt sure of her. Rose was in a torpid state just now, and wished to remain so. She would not stir up trouble, especially as it might be highly inconvenient for Ives if she did, for once the Squire and Mrs Broughton became alarmed, they would put pressure on him to dismiss Owen. He was essential to Pleasance and would be for some time ahead. Ives would resist, and there would be a good deal of friction. Rose would come in for her share of the blame, especially from her irate husband, and as she loved Ives considerably more than he loved her, that would make her very unhappy.

But Christobel, though percipient beyond her years, was not heartless, and she suffered a pang of remorse. Poor Rose. She ought not to be worried or made unhappy at this time. She had her child to think of. In spite of all that was now Rose's, Christobel sometimes thought her sister's lot was not enviable. Ives was good to her. He was generous and indulgent, but he often seemed slightly bored with her; and although he was pleased about the expected baby, he did not share Rose's rapture to the same degree. Often he had the appearance of one whose thoughts were far away.

In a sudden access of sisterly affection, Christobel said: 'It's all right, Rosy. We shan't do anything rash or wrong. I promise you that. Don't worry. Everything will come right in the end.'

Rose could not imagine how that would be brought about, unless Owen and Christobel tired of each other, but that of course was possible. Chrissy was so young. Girls of seventeen must often fancy they were in love. Probably this was no more than a romantic friendship, and Chrissie would have other such friendships, before she met someone who would make her a suitable husband.

Their conversation was interrupted by Caroline who arrived in her carriage. These days, it was thought that Rose should not be left much alone, which she would have been had her family not lived so near. Her mother and elder sister took turn in keeping her company. Ives was much occupied, planning for his new home, supervising gardeners, stocking the stables with horses from which he proposed to breed, and with others which were to be trained for racing, an industry which had brought wealth to the owners of Pleasance in Tudor days. There was also the park; so overgrown that it was almost impenetrable, and in order to bring it back to its old stately beauty, many trees would have to be felled. Woodmen in the district were scarce, and Ives was not above taking his share of the work, now that the spring was almost here.

Sometimes Rose walked across the gardens to watch him and the men he employed, but now that she was becoming heavy and languid, the exercise was too much for her, and she preferred to drive out in her carriage.

As a rule, Caroline did not come over to the Dower House when Christobel was there; she had sufficient to keep her occupied with her household and her social activities, and both girls greeted her with some surprise as the maid opened the drawing-room door for her.

'Don't get up, my dear Rose,' said Caroline quickly to her eldest daughter, but accepting the chair which Christobel vacated for her. 'I drove over to bring you some news; sad news unfortunately, and I only hope you will not be unduly upset. This is a time when you are obliged to be selfish, and to think of yourself first and foremost. Besides, it is not as though you knew the poor man at all well, though naturally you will be distressed for her sake, and for your poor Aunt Hilda who seems to be in a really distracted state, and just when all was going so well with her . . .'

From these disjointed words the two girls could gather little, and Rose said: 'Has anything happened to Sir Rodney – oh, surely not?'

Mrs Talbot had been married for the second time, shortly before Rose's wedding, and in her letters she had been quite ecstatic over the fine country estate of which she was now the mistress, and eloquent about Sir Rodney's perfections as a husband.

'No – oh, no – thank heaven. It's that poor, unfortunate Lavinia. Her husband has died suddenly in Paris. Pneumonia, your aunt writes. His lungs were far from sound, it seems, and he was carried off with tragic swiftness. Your aunt has gone to Paris to be with Lavinia, who is prostrate.'

Rose exclaimed in horror: 'Oh, Mama, how terrible! Livvy was so much in love with him. Well, of course she was, or she wouldn't have eloped with him.'

'Poor, reckless child,' sighed Caroline. 'Even if he hadn't died . . . I can tell you now, girls, what your Aunt Hilda has suspected for some time, and has confided to me in her letters. The marriage was most ill-advised and was bound to turn out badly. I would not say that Mr Swan married Livvy for her money, but he was a weak, unstable character, and the possession of it must have gone to his head. He has gambled away nearly all of that substantial fortune, and now Livvy is very poorly placed, and will be largely dependent on her step-father's generosity. Fortunately, as your aunt says, he is a most kind and generous man, but this is a blow to them, not only on Lavinia's account, but on their own. However, as your aunt writes the first thing to do is to see the poor young widow restored to normal health. Under the circumstances it is really providential that there is no child of the marriage.'

Rose was so genuinely shocked that she was speechless, but Christobel said: 'Sometimes a child is born after the father dies.'

'There is no prospect of that, mercifully. Livvy will at least have no encumbrances. Your aunt will bring her back to England as soon as she is fit to travel, and after a while the least I can do is to offer to have Livvy for a long visit. We have room and to spare, and horror-struck though I was when I heard of her elopment, I was always fond of her. She was much attached to you, Rose.'

'Yes, when I was younger,' said Rose. 'Afterwards we hadn't much in common. Livvy is so musical, and as you know, Mama, I have very little ear for it.'

'Which I once deplored, my dear, though it is unimportant now. To be able to play on the pianoforte is a valuable accomplishment for any girl. However, you have become excellent at managing a household, and I have no doubt you will be an equally good mother.' And then before Rose had the chance to bask in her mother's approval, her eye fell on the unfinished baby's garment, and she said with dismay: 'Oh, my child, what stitches! In such tiny tucks they should be almost invisible. You had better let me unpick them and do the work over again.'

With the utmost readiness Rose handed over the baby's robe.

❋ CHAPTER 10 ❋

Rose was confined in July, and gave birth to a daughter, to Caroline's disappointment. A boy would have been more warmly welcomed as a grandchild; but Rose was content with her baby and Ives, who contemplated a large family, thought it would be time enough to be disappointed when Rose had produced as many daughters as she had sisters. It was a pleasure to him that late summer to see his wife looking well and pretty again. She had been in a poor state of health during the last weeks of her pregnancy and it had been a difficult birth. But since the baby was born, Rose had picked up and Ives was indulgent over the matter of new gowns and bonnets, and to celebrate his daughter's birth gave her another bracelet to add to an already considerable collection.

An excellent nurse for the little girl was engaged, and Rose was once more companionable to her husband. Pleasance was now taking shape as a house built on the same lines as its predecessor, with grey pilastered façade and long windows opening upon the terrace. In style it was a mingling of that which had been most attractive in all the successive periods. Rose had not visualized a castle but that, it seemed to her, was what Pleasance would be, with its branching wings to north and south, its turrets and twisted chimneys. At one time she had secretly wanted a more modern house, but now she was spellbound by such grandeur, and naïvely said so.

'Goose,' said Ives, pinching a cheek once more round and dimpled, 'you must have had some picture of it in your mind. You have seen the old engravings, and knew I wanted it to be much the same.'

'I didn't think it was possible, and there *are* differences; those carved balconies for instance, and the rounded shape of them, carrying out the style of the turrets.'

'That was Owen's idea. He suggested various alterations and additions when he was working on the plans, and all of them were excellent. He has more than a touch of genius, and will, I doubt not, net fame for himself. One day, Pleasance will be cited as an example of his best work. I've been lucky throughout, ever since I left Virginia. All the prizes have been lavished on me. First you, then Pleasance, and Owen Allen to boot.'

'The one blemish being that I haven't given you a son as a first-born.'

'Do not regret that, for I am enthralled with my lovely little daughter. I had no idea that a babe of a few months old could be so enchanting.'

'She *is* a sweet poppet,' Rose agreed, 'and she's very like you with those great dark eyes.'

'We must see that she has a happy childhood. I'd be sorry to see those dark eyes as miserable as mine must sometimes have looked.'

'But of course she'll be happy. Why not? Christobel and I were, and the younger ones are now. Mama may be rather strict but she was always loving and kind. Weren't your parents kind to you?'

'I only remember my mother as an invalid,' said Ives. 'I don't know what was wrong with her, except that she was very unhappy, poor thing, and went into a decline when I was only a few years old. Of my father I saw little as a child. He was a coarse, hard character; cruel and unfaithful to my mother, piling up dollars through his successful dealings as a slave trader, and uninterested in me until I was almost a man. The fact was he was passionately enamoured of a half-caste woman. She had Circassian blood in her, and was beautiful in a savage voluptuous way. My father coveted her when she belonged to a friend of his. He bought her and made her his mistress while my mother still lived. That finally broke my mother, poor soul, for she had been an heiress and delicately reared. Her jewels were taken from her, and this woman, this slave was decked out in them. She presided at my father's table as hostess, he flaunted her in the face of all who knew him. By the time my mother died, he had scarcely one reputable friend, and after she died for a time he was like a madman. He gave Jessamy, as he called her, her freedom, gave her everything except his name. She was no more faithful to him than he had been faithful to my mother, and when she died suddenly there were those who said my father had had her poisoned. If so, it was no more than she deserved. By that time I had left school and could be of use on the estate. My father aged rapidly in the next years, and by the time I was in my twenties I was the virtual master. I detested the entire régime, and when at last my father died I sold the plantation as you know, giving the slaves their freedom.'

What a lonely, desolate life, thought Rose, sympathetically pressing his arm. She said : 'Our child, our children if we have others, shall never be unloved and unhappy, and as for you, you are perfect for me, and I am for you, and we shall never be unfaithful to each other.'

They were alone in the great hall of the new Pleasance, which as yet was open to the sky and scattered with rubble; Ives took her in his arms and kissed her. Vibrant, loving and passionate, she pressed to him, but even as he caressed her, Ives could smile half-pityingly. He had married her and he did not regret it. As a wife and hostess she was satisfactory; in love no girl could have been more responsive, but though Rose believed that all was ideal, he knew that there were depths in him which she could never satisfy. Perhaps no woman could, for he was very fond of Rose.

Putting her from him, he said : 'Has it occurred to you that Owen and Christobel take every opportunity to be together?'

Rose, brought back to earth too soon, sighed resentfully. Christobel was one of the worries which she was glad to dismiss from her mind. 'Oh, I know it, and it's madness, or at least Papa and Mama would say so; but Chrissie says their love for each other is unalterable, and that if necessary she will wait for him until she is of age. As she is only seventeen it's impossible to take seriously.'

'In most cases I should agree, but Christobel is an unusual girl, and Owen is an unusual man. They will, if necessary, be patient. You and I, my love, would have found that torture, but they are different.'

'You mean they are cold-blooded? But that is a poor kind of love.'

Ives shook his head but did not try to explain. Christobel with her love of learning, her vivid imagination, the something fey and strange about her, was not seductive to him, though he realized that she had an ethereal beauty. Far from being cold, her love when released would be as bright and fierce as a flame, but both she and Owen had the power to hold intensity at bay. Owen had chivalry. Christobel was fastidious, and it would never occur to her to be provocative; since this could only make the waiting time more difficult for both of them.

'It is,' said Rose with an air of wisdom at which Ives smiled, 'a great danger to love deeply. Many women must suffer when they give their hearts and souls to one who is unworthy. I am sure that poor Livvy was wretched before her husband died.'

'It's surprising she had so little influence over him,' said Ives. 'He looked a weakling, and no doubt was.'

'But such husbands must be the most difficult of all to influence. Livvy probably wrung promise after promise from him not to gamble, but she could not make him keep his promises, or give a strong character to one who succumbed to every temptation. She would have been better off with a really bad man who loved her so much he was determined to reform. Even if he did not, I suspect it is men of that type who are the successful gamblers, and such a one might have added to Livvy's fortune instead of depleting it.'

Ives, who still found Rose's mingled naïvety and shrewdness diverting, laughed aloud. 'So he might, and such a man might have had a strong constitution and would not have died of pneumonia, leaving his wife to face disaster.'

'Lavinia made a very bad choice for all her sophistication,' said Rose. 'Aunt Hilda would be glad if she were invited to stay at Derevale, and Mama asked me how I would feel about it. I said I must talk to you, and would then let her know.'

'My dear girl, what have I to do with it?'

'You were very taken with her once, Ives. I have not spoken of that to Mama, but before you met me, Aunt Hilda was writing about it, saying she hoped Livvy would marry you.'

'But that is all over and done with long ago,' said Ives. 'I fancied myself in love with Lavinia who would have none of me. I soon got over it, and there is nothing so dead as a dead love. It was Lavinia's freshness, her unspoilt youth which attracted me, and that she has no longer. Her mother has said in her letters that she is greatly altered.'

'Yes, she has. She laments because poor Livvy has lost her freshness as well as her money, and although she does not say so in actual words, she evidently doubts that she will ever marry again. But of course it is far too soon to think of that. She will be in deep mourning for months.'

'Your mother must do as she pleases about inviting her to Derevale. Could she possibly have thought you might be jealous?'

'I dare say she did. She said it might be awkward, which is a word that covers a lot. Mama has always been very conscious of awkwardnesses, and very clever at avoiding them. It makes life easier for herself and other people.'

'Well, my pet, if you think it would be awkward to have Lavinia staying near, you must say so,' Ives replied. 'One way or the other it will make no difference to me.'

He was entirely sincere, for although he had thought of Lavinia with nostalgia, that had been in the early months of marriage. Then, visioning her as sensuously happy with her husband, he had nursed an irrational anger. But when Joseph Swan died and Lavinia's unhappiness was revealed; when ill, widowed and badly off, she had been brought home to her mother's country house, Ives had suffered a change of heart. Thinking of it, it seemed to him that it had been brought about by the deterioration in his imaginative vision of Lavinia. He had seen her always as the beautiful, wealthy girl, courted and adored, exquisite in every detail. Even her maddening indifference to him had been part of her allure. She had been the Snow Princess, and as such inviolate and unattainable. Joseph's needy, dispirited widow bore no resemblance to her.

'Then I think it would be only kind, only charitable to invite her to stay,' Rose decided, 'and I'm sure Mama really wants to, in order to oblige Aunt Hilda. Poor Livvy is an encumbrance to her, and to Uncle Rodney. Of course they thought she was off their hands, and now it seems as though they may have her always. It's only fair that close relations should help if they can.'

Ives indifferently agreed, not guessing that Rose was happily anticipating this visit, and for most unworthy reasons. Lavinia had been so superior, so patronizing, that it would not be unpleasant to extend patronage in her turn.

She treated me like a country cousin, thought Rose, and so I was, I don't deny it, but she made me *feel* it. All that talk about not eating cakes and sweets, and looking me over with a sarcastic smile, because my clothes were not made in London, and I was too plump, or so she thought. There was Ives too – he wasn't good enough for her; not romantic or musical, not to be compared with her poor, silly, spendthrift Joseph, and now the difference, with this wonderful house which will soon be our home, and even the Dower House is charming. She'll be forced to realize how important Ives is, and she can't help but admire my clothes and the beautiful jewels Ives has given me. She hasn't even a child – though I suppose that poor as she is, she's thankful for that.

Rose lost no time in telling her mother that dear Livvy should certainly be invited to stay at Derevale, and for as long as she wished, or as long as Caroline wished.

'If it's rather a tax on you, dearest Mama, to have a visitor who according to Aunt Hilda's letters is a semi-invalid, we can take her at the Dower House for part of the time; and while she's with you, Chrissie will be able to entertain her,' said Rose.

That, too, might be a blessing, she reflected, for it would give her sister less opportunity to be with Owen, a fact which Christobel was quick to recognize.

'I know very little about Lavinia,' she told her lover when next they met. 'It must be five or six years since she last stayed with us. I had scarcely anything to do with her, for Rose and she were always together. Rose was Papa's pet, and she was a real show-off with her horse-riding and being able to shoot, and so much Papa's companion. I do remember that Lavinia seemed to admire her tremendously, but when Rose was in London, just at the time Lavinia eloped, all was changed. She was beautiful and important and poor Rose was nowhere. It wounded her pride, and I suppose it's natural she should feel some pleasure because the tables are turned. It's as natural that I should be selfish and wish Lavinia would stay away, for I shall be the one expected to see she's not bored or neglected, and in return she may notice that you and I love each other, and then if she told Mama . . .'

Owen who had red hair, green eyes and a freckled skin, with the rather unexpected conjunction of fine, classical features, was slightly taller than Ives, and had the effect of making Christobel, though she was above the average in height, look fragile and even younger than her seventeen years. As they walked through the park together, they moved with such leisurely serenity that the deer grazing there did not leap away but only turned their heads to gaze at them incuriously. Not that any untamed animal was afraid of Christobel. She had a way with them, and with the birds whose notes she could imitate. They would fly to her and sit on her shoulders and her outstretched hands.

'Would it greatly matter if your mother did find out?' asked Owen. 'What could she or anyone do? We are not planning to elope as your cousin did. We are resigned to waiting years, and who can prevent us?'

'Papa or Mama could stop us meeting,' said Christobel. 'They could even send me away, though I'm sure I don't know where.'

'There's no need for that. When Pleasance is finished, I shall be no longer living here, and we shall seldom meet, though I dare say Ives will occasionally ask me down to spend a few days.'

'Well, they could stop that,' said Christobel.

'I doubt it. Nobody dictates to him, and I think your parents will soon recognize that our eventual union is inevitable.'

'Rose is sure they will be thunderstruck, and of course most disapproving. I feel upset about Lavinia coming here. I have – what is the old saying? A pricking of my thumbs.'

'Are you such a witch then?' and Owen laughed.

Christobel took this seriously. She said: 'I believe people might have said I was a hundred years ago. I do sometimes seem to have an extra sight, and I know – I know it would be better for Lavinia to keep away, for her sake as well as for everyone's sake. I know too, that we'd all be happier if the park were to be left as it is now. Every time a tree is felled I feel a kind of horror.'

She leant against him and Owen caressingly smoothed her dark hair. He said: 'Why in the world should you feel that way about the park? It needs thinning out. It's so dense one has difficulty in thrusting a way through it. There's only this one path and it's uncomfortably narrow, whereas there should be grassy glades and walks. It will be a slow job as woodmen are so scarce.'

'I dare say it's necessary,' Christobel agreed reluctantly, 'though it will be a shock to the deer and the squirrels and the birds. Ives talks of shooting some of the deer. He says many people still eat venison, consider it a luxury. How can they? Such beautiful creatures.'

Owen had a more practical mind, but he did not argue with her or point out that in the long, severe winters many of the deer died of starvation. Christobel went on: 'The birds will find other homes, other forests in which to nest, but the trees have such grace and beauty. I hate to think they will be felled and used as logs for fires, and sometimes I feel I'm not the only one to hate it. The old shades – those who once owned Pleasance and loved it, have been left undisturbed for so many years – can't you imagine how they resent it now?'

Her lover did not laugh at her or answer teasingly, but said with all seriousness: 'If there are such shades, won't they be glad to see Pleasance restored to its former glory?'

'I don't know. Perhaps this new building will obliterate them, as they have never before been obliterated. They will have no part in your creation. Not even you understand how I fear this place, though it's too beautiful to hate. I would never come here and walk in the park alone, though I'm not afraid with you; perhaps because you are so good. Against real goodness, evil has no chance.'

Owen was as much amused as astonished: 'Don't try to turn me into a saint, my darling.'

'You're not a saint, but a good person – nothing base in you, Owen, whether of the flesh or the spirit. Loyal and kind and with so much love to give. When I think of what you are, I know I'm the luckiest girl in the world. If you lived here, the old evil beings might fade away, but they won't while Ives is in possession.'

'But he's a fine fellow,' Owen protested. 'Energetic, generous, kind-hearted. Why don't you like him?'

'I do like him sometimes, but I wish he really loved Rose. He's no more than fond of her, amused by her. If they were happy above the average, they would have nothing to fear; but Ives is a divided sort of person. I admire him as you do – especially for his attitude to the slavery in America. And then there's his strong will and his courage; but all his virtues are – are earthy. I can't explain it any better, but I feel that Pleasance will be stronger than he is.' Once more Christobel shivered, and then said: 'Let us go back. Rose is always on edge when I'm away for too long, especially if she knows I am with you.'

❋ CHAPTER 11 ❋

The winter passed pleasantly if rather monotonously. The work on Pleasance was slowed down, for from December to March the weather was more than usually severe. Heavy falls of snow and hard frosts made outside work impossible, and because of the glacier-like condition of the roads, social life was at a standstill. The horses could not keep a footing unless a mixture of sand and salt was sprinkled, therefore visiting was limited to families who lived near to each other. On many days a desultory idleness prevailed, and as by Ives's orders the men were paid even though they did little, they at least would have said that the Arctic weather was not without its advantages.

Rose did not fret overmuch for she had plenty to occupy her. To be the mistress of a household was still a novelty to her. She was in love with her husband and charmed with her daughter who was now becoming more interesting as she acquired individuality. Lavinia, who had received an invitation to stay at Derevale Manor for as long as she pleased, had written gratefully, but had pleaded ill health. She did not, she said, feel equal to even a slight exertion, and could not immediately face the journey. If dear Aunt Caroline would allow her to take advantage of the invitation in the spring, then she would be delighted.

'She probably thinks it would be extremely dull and quiet here in the winter,' said Rose crossly. 'I don't believe she's as debilitated in health as she makes herself out to be. Aunt Hilda says that the doctors can find nothing wrong with her, and recommend that she should make an effort.'

'The poor girl has sustained a great shock,' said Caroline more sympathetically. 'It takes time to pick up after such a bereavement.'

Christobel continued to hope that Lavinia would stay away for ever.

'One thing,' said Rose, 'Livvy will be out of deep mourning by the time she is here in the spring. It would have been melancholy for her, and perhaps for all of us at Christmas, for one couldn't have expected her to take any part in the festivities, and it would have seemed heartless to give even small family parties. But now she can with propriety begin to recover.'

'It's hypocritical that a person in Lavinia's position has to pretend to grieve,' remarked Christobel with scorn. 'Aunt Hilda says that almost from the outset she was unhappy in her marriage. I dare say she's already thinking that her one hope now is to captivate one of her old admirers.'

'She may not find that so easy,' said Rose. 'Poor Livvy.'

It was easy to feel sad about one whose folly had ruined her life, though she might not as yet fully realize it. It would take time for a girl who had been such a success, so much admired, to grasp that she was no longer fascinating or desirable.

'Uncle Rodney can't be expected to keep her for ever,' said Rose, 'but I dare say she could give music lessons – singing also, and with the little money that she has left, she would then be self-supporting.'

'Rose! You know Aunt Hilda wouldn't permit it. She would think it reflected very badly on her, married to someone as rich as Uncle Rodney.'

'How could she prevent it if Livvy insisted? She couldn't

prevent her elopement could she?'

'No, but that was what Livvy wanted,' said Christobel.

'Well, why shouldn't she want to be independent? I'm sure I should if I were in her situation.'

Mingled amusement and scorn gleamed in Christobel's eyes as they rested on her sister; so richly dressed, so jewelled, so pampered. Rose was again *enceinte* and was none too well pleased. She was willing to have further children, but there would be only eleven months between little Esme and the second arrival, and Rose had counted on at least a year's respite before the start of her next pregnancy, though to her relief she was feeling surprisingly well. There was a complete absence of the nausea and weariness which she had previously experienced.

'Marriage has its drawbacks,' said Rose petulantly. 'I'd set my heart on being a companion to Ives, but how can I be when he is so active and I shall soon be waddling again?' Her sense of humour, not so strong nowadays, for it was often submerged by self importance, induced a giggle. 'Some women are lucky, they look presentable to the end, but I was huge with Esme as you know, and I'll probably look even worse with this one. It means an entirely new wardrobe just for a few months.'

'But you have the clothes you wore for Esme.'

'I have not.' Rose's smile was impish. 'It occurred to me that something such as this might happen – another baby too quickly – so I took care to give my old things away to that Mrs Bruges in the village, who is having her eighth, poor soul, and was thankful for all I could pass on to her. The least I can do for Ives is to look as agreeable as possible, and this new dressmaker, Miss Crowe, who has set up in Mellor is really very clever, as of course she would be for she was apprenticed to a Court dressmaker in London who made poor Queen Adelaide's maternity clothes. Miss Crowe, who must be fifty if she's a day, remembers sewing on hundreds of crystal beads by hand, she says, for one of her loose evening gowns. She was so sorry for the poor Queen whose hopes all came to nothing. It's said though, that she's as fond of Victoria as she would be of her own daughter.'

Rose who enjoyed talking about royalty, prattled on, and

continued to do so even when Ives joined them, though he was mildly bored. Indulgent however, for he readily told Rose to order all she required, and agreed that it would be a good idea for her to give a dinner-party for those friends and neighbours who had recently entertained them, while she still looked no more than becomingly plump.

Rose began to plan happily, saying she would have the party before Lavinia arrived. It could be only a small one, for the dining-table at the Dower House would not seat more than a dozen.

'How different when Pleasance is finished,' she said. 'Then we can give a tremendous house-warming. I do think a really big dance would be more exciting than a dinner-party, and less trouble in the long run. Did Owen tell you, Chrissie, that there's to be a musician's gallery at one end of the banqueting hall? Just as there was in Tudor days, though much grander. It's to be elegantly carved and gilded. Dancing always draws the younger people and perhaps this could be fancy dress, with a band hired from London. Something people hereabouts would talk of for years.'

'You're looking a long way ahead, Pet,' Ives said. 'Even the roof is not on as yet.'

'The men are so slow, or have been. With the spring here the foreman must insist that they work full time. Otherwise what's the good of having a foreman? The lovely silver-tiled roof with the gilded weather vanes will look superb. I'm so tired of seeing just beams and acres of tarpaulin. I was saying so to the Vicar the other day, but he said patience was needed always over a great undertaking. He has a wonderful opinion of you, darling.'

Ives seemed amused, and even more so when Rose continued innocently: 'But of course it's because you are so generous. It must have quite stunned the poor man when you headed the subscription list for church repairs with five hundred pounds, and on top of that said you would be responsible for the building of the new Parish Hall.'

'On the distinct understanding,' said Ives, 'that his Reverence does not start on it until the very last touch has been put to Pleasance. The stipulation was necessary, or he'd have been luring our men away to get on with his project.'

'But my dear, how ungrateful! Besides he would not pay them half as well . . . though I forgot, I suppose you will be paying them, though surely not such high rates. A Parish Hall is only a simple building.'

'Which means more straightforward work – less risky.'

'Is the work on Pleasance dangerous?' asked Christobel.

'It's not devoid of danger, though nothing out of the way I should have thought. The word is going round that it's an unlucky job. There have been three accidents, and the last one when the poor chap fell from the turret to the floor beneath was serious. He shouldn't have been up on the high scaffolding: too old. In his sixties I've heard since. He had a giddy fit and little wonder.'

'I had no idea poor Anders was badly hurt,' said Rose with concern, for she had known this village family all her life.

'At first it was not thought to be too bad, but the doctors now doubt if he'll ever walk again. I've had the best advice for him, but go to hospital he will not. The most I can give is the comfort of promising he will never want, and the poor chap himself has no blame for me, since it seems that the foreman forbade him to try the heights, which stung Anders who thought himself as good as the best of them, in spite of his age.'

'Then really, it was his own fault,' said Rose, 'which of course doesn't make one the less sorry. I must drive down to the village and see Mrs Anders. They're a most respectable family. Mama took the eldest girl and trained her for service when she left school, and for a time she was a kitchen maid at home, but then she married and went to live farther north. But why do the workmen talk of bad luck in a general way? There must often be such accidents.'

'Perhaps three is a high proportion,' said Ives. 'A part of the old wall fell on one man, and the boarding of a floor gave way beneath another. Both were puzzling, as the wall had been tested and judged sound, and the boards of that particular room were only just laid. After the wall fell, Owen and I decided to do away with all that remained, though I was sorry about that, as I'd a sentimental fancy to keep what I could of the old building, not merely to build on its foundations. As for the floor collapse, that was due to bad workmanship, though it hasn't been discovered which of the men were responsible. Fortunately in those cases the injury was no more than a broken leg and a mild concussion. There's no doubt though that amongst the villagers Pleasance has the reputation for being uncanny and – an absurd word, but I can't think of a better one – malevolent.'

Rose said petulantly: 'It's too stupid. I've heard the talk myself. The maids chatter, and though naturally I don't encourage it, it seemed better to know exactly what was being said. I asked Ada one evening when she was doing my hair, and she said that only the high wages induced the men to work on the new building. For years, it seems, the villagers have shunned going near the place after dusk.'

'Why?' asked Christobel. 'What makes them frightened?'

'Nothing actual, so far as I could find out, and I can guess how it all started. Parents, as their boys and girls grew up, invented frightening fairy tales, because the grounds being untended and with no house to overlook them, were favoured by courting couples, and then trouble resulted. Mothers impressed on their girls that the place was haunted, and so kept them out of moral danger. Ada did have some silly story about mysterious lights seen, and footsteps and voices heard, but it was only what her mother and grandmother had told her. She said the boldest of the village girls could not be tempted to go near the place, which of course from one point of view is a very good thing, though now that we intend to live there, it makes it rather unpleasant for us.'

Ives had listened to this with more than idle attention, and he said: 'Have you found it difficult to keep servants here, at the Dower House?'

'Oh, dear me, no! They all seem quite happy, but then the Dower House is not exactly in the grounds, and there never has been any history attached to it.'

'Well, all that will be forgotten when we are once more in residence,' said Ives, 'and even allowing for local superstition, there's no basis for horrific stories. One might well think some notorious murder had occurred at Pleasance.'

'In such an old house it would be odd if there hadn't been

a few tragedies,' Christobel remarked, 'especially as it existed in such troubled times. There may have been murders, Ives, which were never discovered.'

'I assure you, my dear, we have unearthed no skeletons – not so much as a handful of bones, and they couldn't have escaped us. The foundations of the house were put to every known test before Owen and the surveyor passed it.'

'You don't have to bury people in the foundations, if a murder has never been suspected,' Christobel retorted. 'And it needn't have been even that. People can die for lack of being warned.'

Rose shivered: 'Oh, do let us talk of something more cheerful,' she said plaintively. 'I'm sure it's not good in my condition to brood on horrors.'

'Indeed it is not,' Ives concurred. 'Suppose you have a glass of Madeira, my love, to revive you. It will give you an appetite for your luncheon.'

'It's very rarely I haven't an appetite when I'm in this state. One mercy is that I shall have presented you with your son and heir before we are living at Pleasance. I'm convinced it will be a boy this time.'

Christobel's gaze was fixed thoughtfully on Ives as he got up to ring the bell, and when a servant arrived, ordered the wine to be brought. Although he had made every effort to win local popularity, she did not believe it was of excessive importance to him. He courted it because he was determined on a certain way of life, and had come to England with that fixed plan in his mind. He had not, of course, counted on acquiring Pleasance; that, with Rose attached to it, had fallen into his possession by a stroke of luck. In Virginia, as the owner of a large plantation, he would have lived in solitary grandeur, shunned by many because of his father's reputation, disliked because of his disapproval of slavery; a pariah in fact. In England he was set on having all the advantages attached to wealth and property; of being a leader of the community, even though members of it might strike him as dull-witted and insufferably complacent. Christobel could not fathom Ives's true nature, but as she had told Owen she sensed that he was a divided person, sometimes despising what he sought to gain. But he did not despise Pleasance. The place would be ideal for his purpose; so in most aspects was Rose ideal as a wife, her family being well thought of, and she adoring and biddable; more so possibly than Pleasance, though both were Ives's possessions. Were those old shades at war amongst themselves? Christobel wondered. Did some welcome the restoration, and others oppose it? She smiled at her fanciful thoughts, only half-believing in them.

❈ CHAPTER 12 ❈

Lavinia came to Derevale in the early spring, and from the first it was disconcerting to her relations who had been prepared to pity and patronize her.

Caroline Broughton was somewhat shocked to find that after a bare year of widowhood, her niece had discarded her mourning, for really, she thought, one could not connect the delicate pastel shades that Lavinia wore with any semblance of bereavement, even though the prevailing shades might be dove and pearl grey, or lavender shading to shell-pink. The criticism was not immediate, for Caroline's last wish was to be critical. Her attitude before meeting Lavinia again was sympathetic. She was prepared to listen to her woes and to give advice. They must all be very kind to poor Lavinia, she insisted, and make her warmly welcome.

Christobel accompanied her mother when Caroline ordered the carriage, and said she intended to meet the train which would bring Lavinia to Derevale. Train journeys to country people were still something of a novelty, and the nearest station was seven miles away. The journey from London had been slow, the carriages were cold, draughty and uncomfortable, but Lavinia seemed to have been well looked after. Her mother had sent a maid with her, as she considered it improper for a young woman to travel alone, and really, thought Caroline, her niece might still have been an important heiress from the way that middle-aged woman fussed over her.

Lavinia had been provided with a luncheon basket which contained cold chicken and fruit and a bottle of champagne. There had been a foot-warmer and a fur rug, and the maid carried her expensive white leather dressing-case. Although Joseph Swan had squandered her fortune she wore a sealskin cape, and an impressive half-hoop of diamonds glittered above the broad gold band of her wedding ring.

Embraced by Caroline as she stepped down from the train to the platform, Lavinia assured her that Marble, her maid, would be staying for only a few days to 'settle her in'. Poor, darling Mama worried so about her health, and it was true that she had had a nasty cough throughout the winter, which had only recently disappeared.

Christobel, surveying an elegant young woman with little resemblance to the cousin she remembered, could not sort out her first impressions. She finally decided that although only twenty-three, Lavinia did not look a girl. But then of course she wasn't; she had been a wife and was now a widow; she had been in love and then disillusioned. She had been rich, and now she was poor.

During that homeward drive, Christobel discovered that Lavinia had an unusual voice and a singularly attractive smile. The voice was a low contralto, the smile slightly lop-sided. Heavy white lids gave her eyes a sleepy expression.

Caroline was put out because of Marble. Hilda, she thought, should have warned her; but on the other hand ought she not to have expected her? None of her daughters would have been allowed to travel unescorted. Caroline was faintly but uncomfortably ashamed of herself because she had assumed that Lavinia after her reckless marriage, her months in Paris with a gambler husband and the disappearance of her fortune, needed no such conventional chaperonage.

Marble, the maid, was so superior in manner and appearance that Caroline did not venture to suggest she should sit beside the coachman, though it was a fine enough day. Instead, she sat primly upright, next to Christobel, with her back to the horses, holding Lavinia's dressing-case on her knee. Lavinia herself, looked as useless, helpless and exquisite as a piece of fragile china. Adversity appeared to have made no impression on her, thought Caroline with irritation, but could not deny that her manner was sweetly affectionate, as she said that she was so thankful to be in the beautiful country for a while. Yes, of course her step-father's estate was in a country district, but the winter had been spent in London, and the town house though delightful was rather cramped. It was a pity perhaps that her mother had sold the Kensington house, but she had never cared for it, and Sir Rodney's had been large enough until she – his step-daughter – had joined them.

'I have upset all their plans,' Lavinia admitted with a soft sigh, 'but Mama would not hear of my staying on in Paris, though I could have done so. She said the anxiety of thinking of me there, widowed and alone would be more than she could endure, and that I could hear plenty of good music in London.'

'You will miss that here,' Christobel put in. 'The most we have are choir practices.'

It was then that the lop-sided smile was turned upon her. 'But I could not get out much in London because of the fogs, and I make my own music.'

'Of course we have a pianoforte,' said Caroline, trying to remember when the grand in the drawing-room had last been tuned. 'Do you still play much? None of my girls are at all musical, unfortunately.'

'I compose,' said Lavinia. 'I have had quite a few songs published. This was in Paris, but now a London music publisher has started to take an interest.'

Caroline stared at her in amazement. *Why* hadn't Hilda told her? Lavinia read the unuttered question and supplied the answer. 'Mama thinks it is far from *comme il faut* for a lady of quality to earn money,' she said.

'But do you – do you really?' asked Christobel, alertly interested.

'A little – and some day it will be more than a little. Chrissie, how pretty you are. Is she the beauty of the family, Aunt Caroline?'

Christobel blushed and Caroline frowned. 'We all think that Chrissie has a pleasant face,' she said repressively, 'but her carriage leaves much to be desired. Unlike Rose who holds herself well. That and her colouring have always been much admired.'

'I am sure of it,' Lavinia said politely. 'How is Rose? In different ways as much has happened to her as to me. I do so want to see her little girl. She must be a great pet with you all.'

'Indeed, yes. Esme is a sweet child,' said Caroline, and added in a low voice, not wishing either the coachman or Marble to hear her, 'in the autumn there will be an increase.'

'Why, Aunt Caroline, that's wonderful,' said Lavinia. 'Only isn't it rather soon?'

'Rose thought so at first,' Caroline admitted, 'but now as she very sensibly says, the two children being so much of an age will be great companions.'

❋ CHAPTER 13 ❋

Rose was spending the afternoon at her old home in order to be there to welcome Lavinia on her arrival. Greetings mingled with commiseration as the burgeoning young wife embraced the fragile widow, but Lavinia, though she did not crudely repel sympathy, seemed to endure rather than to welcome it. A flood of tears would have shown more sensibility thought Rose, as Lavinia murmured that she was very tired, and Caroline at once said that she would show her to her room, where she could if she wished rest for a while. Tea could be brought up to her, Caroline added kindly.

Rose and Christobel, the former quite pleased to have the opportunity to criticize Lavinia, were in the drawing-room when Caroline joined them, looking somewhat taut, for although the room prepared for Lavinia was very comfortable, and the afternoon sun was pouring in through the windows, Marble had at once gone down on her knees before the grate to set light to the sticks and coals laid there. Mrs Swan, she said, was one to feel the cold, and it was much bleaker here than in London. Caroline had with difficulty repressed her annoyance. Bedroom fires made a great deal of extra work, and at Derevale once the winter was past, they were allowed only in times of illness.

Overhearing the end of a remark by Rose gave Caroline an excuse to vent her irritation. 'My dear, it is unkind to be critical,' she said. 'After that tedious train journey, poor Lavinia cannot be expected to look her best. You should have more charity, Rose.'

'But all I said was that she looked older than twenty-three and was as thin as a broomstick.'

'Not a bit like a broomstick,' Christobel objected. 'Livvy is very graceful. Elegant too. She reminds me of a heroine in a novel.'

'I expect that's how she sees herself,' said Rose tartly. 'Mama, what is all this about the composing of songs and music and getting them published and paid for? Is it true, or is Livvy making it up in order to seem important?'

'Of course she is not making it up, Rose, and she wasn't boasting about it. She said her – er – musical compositions had brought in only a little money as yet. Chrissie, do ring the bell for tea. It's past five o'clock. Your Papa is still out I believe, so there is no necessity to wait.'

'Chrissie says that Aunt Hilda doesn't approve. Why not?' asked Rose, when tea had been brought in and she was munching chocolate cake.

'It's the publicity I expect,' Caroline replied. 'I did say a few words about it to Livvy, but her maid was there unpacking, and I could not speak freely, though Livvy appears to say anything that comes into her head before the woman. She could be stone deaf.'

'That's her arrogance,' said Rose. 'Servants are hardly human to her. I noticed it when I was staying in London. I don't mean that she and Aunt Hilda were disagreeable or unkind to servants, but they seemed almost unaware that they existed. Surely Mama it would be much nicer for Livvy to earn money through her musical gift than to be a governess or a companion. She would have to do something. It would be so unfair to Uncle Rodney to attach herself to them permanently.'

'It would certainly be a trial for them. Many poor gentlewomen are obliged to support themselves by teaching or something of the kind, but Lavinia . . . well, really, it's disconcerting when she talks of barrel-organs.'

'Barrel-organs!' Rose, about to pop a piece of cake into her mouth, sat with it poised in mid-air. 'How in the world did they come into the conversation?'

'Lavinia said that sooner or later they would all be playing her popular songs, and that your aunt would consider it degrading. You see, my dears, it appears they are comic songs, and have already been sung at music-halls in Paris. I fear they may be rather risqué, and that certainly will be most uncomfortable for your poor Aunt Hilda – I mean when it is known that Lavinia composed them.'

Christobel choked on a laugh, and her mother looked at her reproachfully. After a stupefied moment Rose said: 'I can't believe it – that isn't Livvy's style. She was always so serious about music; talked about it in such a soulful way.'

'Paris may have changed her tastes, Rose. From all one hears it is not a soulful place. If her husband's – er – standards suffered in one way, Livvy's may have suffered in another. As for her songs, it would not matter so much if they were only known on the Continent, but she seems certain there will be English versions.'

'She need not put her own name to them, Mama.'

'No, but these things seem to leak out sooner or later. Celebrity is all very well, and everyone would be proud of Lavinia if her work was – well, an oratorio, but . . . oh dear, she really seems to think that her mother's distress is amusing. I fear Livvy is sadly changed. As a girl she was so fastidious, but since then she has mixed with some very odd people.'

'Had she any choice if those kind of people were her husband's friends?' enquired Christobel.

Rose felt for her mother who looked really worried. It was too bad, thought Rose. Aunt Hilda had always cast her troubles upon poor Mama, who was only a few years older, but was treated rather contemptuously, as dowdy and countrified, though useful on occasions.

'I dare say it's only a flash in the pan,' said Rose. 'People don't become famous so easily.'

'It can happen if a talent is put to an improper use,' replied Caroline. 'According to Livvy, the song which is now popular is about a French girl who is no better than she should be. Livvy says she composed the music first, and intended to make it a pretty song about birds nesting in the spring, but a French music-hall favourite who was friendly with Livvy's husband, said that would never get her anywhere, and as Livvy was badly in need of money to pay a gambling debt of his, a debt of honour, she turned the nesting birds into human beings who were – well they hadn't any right to be nesting together, and then this music-hall woman said she would include it in her repertoire, and it made quite a sensation.'

'Then it was Joseph Swan's fault,' said Christobel. 'Livvy spoilt her song to save him, though I suppose by that time he had already run through her fortune.'

'I very much fear so, though there were a few thousands she was unable to give him. She had the sense to go to a solicitor before she married him, and a Deed was made securing this comparatively small amount to herself and to her children if she had any.'

'Then even at the beginning she couldn't have altogether trusted him,' mused Rose. 'I don't wonder. He was handsome, and Aunt Hilda said once, though of course she had no idea he meant anything to Livvy, that he had great charm and beautiful manners. Poor Livvy, how miserable for her to have made such a marriage, to have been so disillusioned that she can't even mourn her husband.'

'We have no idea how she thinks of him, Rose. Your aunt is sure she was heartbroken when he died. Hilda has done all she could for Livvy. Marble was unpacking the most beautiful clothes, which Livvy says her mother bought for her to wear when she can discard her mourning. I remember that diamond ring too, and the sealskin cape. They both belonged to Hilda. The ring was the one Lavinia's father put on Hilda's finger when they were engaged. I doubt if Joseph Swan thought of giving the poor girl anything. But I suppose she makes excuses for him, wastrel though he was, for that is a woman's way.'

'Not Lavinia's way,' said Christobel positively. 'She detests the very thought of him.'

'Chrissie, really!' Caroline remonstrated. 'That's a dreadful thing to say.'

'How can you possibly know?' Rose demanded.

Christobel was looking slightly dazed. 'It came to me,' she said. 'All in a moment I was sure.'

'That's nonsense, Chrissie.' Caroline was shocked. 'But it's not right for us to have talked before you. I blame myself. I forget how young you still are. Rose is different; not only older but married. The fact is I've had a shock – one of several shocks; hearing about Livvy's music, and then when she told me so coldly and matter-of-factly something of what her life had been with her husband. All I can say is that it should be a lesson to any girl not to marry out of her own class.'

Rose, thinking of Owen Allen, wondered if this was a hurtful remark, but if so Christobel gave no sign of it. She said: 'Mama, it stands to reason she must hate his memory, and somehow I think – I fear it may have made it easy for her to hate others. Poor Livvy, the bottom tumbled out of her world and she resents those who are secure and happy – even her mother. It amuses her to shock. She must have worshipped music and her talent for it, and for him she was forced to spoil something lovely.'

'But she needn't continue to spoil it,' argued Caroline. 'She has *some* money of her own and a mother who will help her. Livvy has a gift, it seems, and she can use it worthily.'

'That may not be so easy,' said Christobel.

Before either her mother or sister could reply, the door opened and Ives came in. Rose glanced at the clock and got hastily to her feet.

'I had no idea it was so late. I am so sorry. I should have been at home by now. I told Harris I would send a message to the stables when I was ready to leave.'

Ives smiled at her kindly as she went to him. 'Never mind, m'dear. It's no more than I expected. You and Lavinia must have had sufficient to talk about to make you forget whether it was noon or midnight. Where is she though? Didn't she arrive?'

'Yes, indeed,' Caroline assured him, 'but Rose has scarcely seen her, as she went straight to her room. She said she would rest and then get into something loose as we shall be *en famille* this evening. Such a fatiguing journey she has had, and she looked so tired.'

'Wilted,' said Rose in a satisfied voice.

'Ah, well, your cousin was never strong and she has been through a bad time,' said Ives indifferently. 'Are you ready to leave, Pet? We have the Pelhams coming to dinner, and shall barely have time to drive home and change. I must postpone meeting Lavinia until tomorrow.'

'Just let me get my bonnet,' said Rose. 'I won't disturb Livvy, Mama. Will you explain to her that I had to get home because we are expecting guests?'

'Of course, my dear, but there's no need to get into a fluster or to run up the stairs. Do remember.'

'I seem to have been remembering to act as an old woman ever since I was married,' pouted Rose, going towards the door.

But it opened before she reached it. There was a soft swish of silk and Lavinia stood there, framed in the dark background of the panelled hall. Rose fell back a step, literally gaping at her. The 'something loose' was an exquisite white chiffon tea-gown, with long, floating, lace-edged sleeves. Lavinia was pale, but it was no longer the pallor of fatigue. The slight hollows beneath her high cheek-bones were accentuated by the style in which her hair was worn, drawn away from brow and ears and massed in ash-blonde coils on the top of her head. Her eyes were brightly luminous. Rose was forced to admit that her cousin was indeed beautiful, though with a different beauty than had been hers as a girl.

'Am I too early?' Lavinia asked. 'I slept and felt so well when I woke up, and I thought . . .'

Caroline who had been as startled as her daughters, bestirred herself. 'My dear child, indeed not. It is we who are late, and should be dressing for dinner; but your uncle has not yet come in and we were talking, and then Ives called for Rose . . .'

'Ives. But of course! I did not notice you in that shadowy corner. What a long time ago it seems . . .'

Lavinia put out a slender white hand, and the loose sleeve fell back from her forearm. Stepping forward, Ives took her hand in his, held it for an instant, and then it was withdrawn. He said : 'It *is* a long time.'

'More than a year and a half,' Lavinia remembered, and sighed : 'Those were happy days.'

Ives wondered. Happy for her because she had been in love, or happy because she had been an inexperienced girl with no knowledge of the cruelty of life? He had forced himself to glance only briefly at her, but his heart was hammering against his ribs. Nothing could be more unlike the forlorn, downcast widow he had expected to see. Nor was she the girlish Lavinia who had flaunted him and scorned him. Much beauty had been added to her since then, much wisdom and much subtlety.

'There will be happier ones for you yet,' he said, and the two girls and their mother accepted that as appropriate. Only Ives was aware that there could be a deeper meaning to his words. Unless Lavinia also understood their significance. But it was madness to think any such thing, and for an instant he was honestly, healthily angry with himself. Her allure, so much greater than it had been two years ago, was not for him. Already he had been given enough. Pleasance. A wife. A child.

Caroline led her niece to a sofa and propped cushions behind her back. Rose, breaking a spell which had held her as it held Ives, left to put on her outdoor clothes. 'My dear,' said Caroline kindly, who saw no more than a wan girl with pathetically big eyes, 'you look as though a breath of air could blow you away.'

'Oh, no, Aunt Caroline, I'm much more solid than you suppose. I have put on weight since leaving Paris. It's this tea-gown which makes me look fragile. It was bought in Paris ages ago and is quite shabby, but you said we should be alone, only the family, and that it wouldn't matter what I wore.'

'Nor does it, though it's a lovely robe which becomes you.'

'I have a fondness for it,' Lavinia admitted, 'but the lace has been much mended.'

She had not glanced again at Ives, but she was acutely

conscious of him, standing there in the background; dark, tall and silent. His eyes had sent her a message. What message? Cool though she seemed she was in a secret ferment. It was as though they had met for the first time; as though a veil had been torn from her eyes and she really saw him. For in the past, she thought, she must have been blind – as blind as foolish.

In those days he had been crazy about her, and she had despised him, considering him a vulgarian, an uncouth creature devoid of sensibility. To her his dark good looks, his essential maleness had held no appeal, obsessed as she was by an altogether different type of man, whose worthlessness and weakness had soon been exposed. Her mother, thought Lavinia, had been the wise one, for she had wanted Ives for her, and had been angrily disappointed when Lavinia pettishly declared that he was dominating and too well-pleased with himself.

And so indeed he might have been, might still be. What matter if it was so? He had reason for it. As for herself, she had been as spellbound as Titania, who had seen all that was desirable in an ass's head. The spell had still been on her when she had heard from her shocked, aggrieved mother that Rose had caught Ives on the rebound and that they were married.

Lavinia had laughed with her husband's arm around her, as together they had read that letter. Disillusionment had not yet crept in. Rose had been welcome to Ives, for all Lavinia cared, and he was welcome to her, with her dairymaid comeliness and her tendency to giggle. But there could be no denying that it was Rose who had walked off with the prize, with a man who was outstanding. He could give her everything she wanted; jewels and costly clothes, and was rebuilding a romantic home for her.

Conflicting emotions drove a slight colour into Lavinia's cheeks so that Rose, when she returned cloaked and bonneted, said kindly: 'Why Livvy, you look better and rested already. Doesn't she, Mama?'

'I believe she does,' Caroline agreed.

Christobel, gazing from one to the other was silent. Rose said: 'It's a shame we have to rush off like this, your first evening, but we shall be late as it is. Luckily you will be here for weeks, so we shall have plenty of time to be together.'

She stooped to put her lips to Lavinia's cheek and Lavinia pressed her hand. 'Yes, indeed, there will be plenty of time,' she agreed.

CHAPTER 14

Rose had never had a more attentive husband than during the next few weeks. When he was not actively engaged at Pleasance, he seemed unable to bear her out of his sight; nor did he seem anxious to visit Derevale Manor. He had, as he pointed out, little or no time to spare during the day, and in the evenings it was better for Rose to go early to bed. It always meant a late night if they dined at Derevale, the Squire being fond of Ives's company.

'Ask your father and mother over here,' Ives suggested. 'Two guests are sufficient for you to entertain these days, and Christobel can keep Lavinia company. No hardship for her, she spends hours here most days.'

'I'm glad to have Chrissie. She's getting much more companionable; but about entertaining, I expect you're right. It is rather an effort,' said Rose, who had no objection to being treated as an interesting invalid, especially by Ives. Though he was rather fussy, she delighted in it. She thought complacently that he really was very much in love with her; more so than when they had been newly wed. As for her, she adored him, and even the trial of having two babies in less than two years was worth the joy of being married to him.

'Livvy has been over twice, with Mama,' Rose said. 'They drove of course, though Livvy says she intends to take up riding again. Then I expect we shall see more of her. Chrissie, of course, nearly always rides. She enjoys the exercise. Livvy has sent to London for the habits she had before she was married. Aunt Hilda is sure to have kept them.'

'She'll find the roads here rough-going after the sedate

trots in Hyde Park,' Ives remarked.

'But it's only a few miles dear, and I'd like to see more of her. Mama so often wants the carriage and Papa has the dog-cart. I could send over one of ours for her, and would if Livvy seemed keener, but she spends much time at the piano, composing. Did I tell you that she bought a spinet and had it sent down from London? Mama gave her the little work-room to use for her music.'

'Generous of her,' Ives commented, 'as she so disapproves of the type of song which may make Lavinia's second fortune.'

'Oh, do you really think so? I mean a real fortune? Livvy, it's true, bought the spinet out of money she'd earned. Royalties she calls them, and now she has a London agent, and a publisher here has given her a contract, but none of us thought she would ever earn more than a hundred or so.'

'My dear child, although I know nothing about music publishing, I should say that "The Nesting Birds" has netted her much more than that. It's already known that she composed both verses and music, and young Raymond Manvers told me the other day that it was on sale in London. In French – so the market will be limited, but a fair lady of his acquaintance, who holds court in a pretty house in St John's Wood, sang it for him, and he says it's a delicious piece of naughtiness.'

'Oh dear! Mr Manvers is very fast I'm afraid.' Rose pursed her lips. 'I know men say he is good company, but his wife has left him and none of our friends will receive him. It would be dreadful if he tried to scrape acquaintance with Livvy; getting a false impression of her I mean. He's not often here, thank goodness and I've heard that he intends to sell Manvers Hall.'

'He might as well for all the good he gets out of the place – boycotted as he is, poor chap,' said Ives.

Rose looked shocked. 'Darling, you can't possibly sympathise with him. He treated poor Harriet Manvers so badly. He did not even pretend to be faithful to her.'

'A dreadful bore of a woman with a long, twitching nose,' was Ives's comment, and Rose giggled.

'It's a shame – poor Harriet. I shouldn't encourage you.

I'm grateful you can't say the same of mine which is nearly a snub.'

'A dear little nose,' said Ives, tweaking it.

'Lavinia's is rather long,' Rose said in a casual voice, 'but I suppose she's a beauty – still. I know I thought she looked beautiful that first evening in her white tea-gown, but since then she has seemed much more ordinary.'

'Much changed from the Lavinia I first knew,' Ives said.

Rose was pleased and snuggled against him, and with his cheek resting on her bright hair, Ives could safely smile. Naturally it would not occur to Rose to read a complimentary meaning into his words. Two years ago, Lavinia had barely emerged from the chrysalis, but now she was as lovely as a white moth. He reflected that if she belonged to him he would not allow her to wear anything *except* white, which intensified the elusive quality of her beauty.

'One evening,' he said, 'I must go over to Derevale and have a game of chess with your father. You won't miss me; not if you take yourself off early to bed, as a good little girl should.'

'You have stayed in with me so many evenings, that I should be indeed selfish if I tried to prevent you,' Rose replied, 'though when I am resting, I like to think you are still near, down here and generally poring over the family history. You've become so interested in it lately.'

'Chrissie inspired the interest,' said Ives, 'and as these various records are mainly about Pleasance, or at all events about those who lived at Pleasance, it's only right the present owner should know something about them.'

'Well, I know *something,*' said Rose, 'but Chrissie reads all kind of secret meanings into those old journals, as though few of the Grentons were exactly what they seemed to be, nor the Pallistiers who followed them.'

'Are any of us quite what we seem to be?' Ives enquired idly.

'Certainly we are. I'm sure I have nothing to hide and nor have you.'

Ives did not contradict her and Rose yawned. The heat of the fire was making her sleepier than usual, and she scarcely needed prompting to admit that she was ready for bed. Ives walked with her to the foot of the stairs, his arm around her shoulders.

'You won't sit up too long, will you?' entreated Rose, who often felt lonely in the big four-poster.

'No, but don't try to force yourself to stay awake. You need all your sleep these days.'

Rose went heavily up the stairs. He was the dearest and the best of husbands, and it was wrong to feel as she sometimes did that she had had too little youth and fun; too little also of being beautiful and desirable to him. All that was needed was patience. In a few months' time the second little one would be here, and she would soon regain her figure and her energy.

Ives returned to the drawing-room, and after a moment pulled a folded piece of paper from his breast pocket. For the last two days he had been mindful of it, changing its hiding place as he changed his suits. Rank folly. Having read what was written on the paper he should have destroyed it, but it was the first communication of any kind that he had had from Lavinia, and he hated to part with it. Not far from Derevale Manor there was an old tree, which some years ago had been struck and blasted by lightning. Now it stood there gauntly, with its spectral arms outstretched. A hollow in the thick trunk provided a useful post-box, and Lavinia had collected several notes from him, which if found by anyone else would not have incriminated him, for they were written or rather printed on plain paper, and were neither addressed nor signed.

When he had told her he would leave messages there, she had neither encouraged nor discouraged him, though she had searched for and found them. There had been little opportunity for them to be alone. Some member of the family was nearly always with her, and it was by the merest chance that they had at last come to an understanding.

Ives and the Squire had been playing chess in the library, but in the middle of a closely contested game, the Squire had been called away to speak to a tenant who had arrived at an untimely hour with an urgent plea. The Squire was a good landlord, and this was the kind of approach he would never disregard. Not expecting to find Ives alone, Lavinia had opened the library door with an apology on her lips. She had come there to find a book which she had been reading earlier in the day.

Every moment of that short meeting lived vividly in Ives's memory and had been dwelt on over and over again. He had stood up so abruptly that his chair had been knocked backwards, and the next instant without a word spoken on either side, Lavinia had been crushed in his arms, his head downbent over hers, his mouth clenched on her mouth. It had been a very delirium of pleasure to discover that she was not only willing but as eager as he, docile as his hands passed over her, not gently but in urgent demand. Save for her gasping sighs they had been silent until a distant door had slammed, and then there was the Squire's voice, talking to the caller before he let him out of the house by a side-door. Quickly Ives had said: 'We must find a time – a place. I'll write to you,' and had described the leafless tree which had suddenly sprung to his memory. She had nodded voicelessly, and he had released her. When the Squire re-entered Ives was hunting for Lavinia's book which had fallen behind a table, and he had put it into her hands. If she had looked slightly rumpled the Squire hadn't noticed it, and no doubt she had smoothed her hair and her dress before rejoining her aunt and Christobel.

Now with renewed pleasure Ives unfolded the crumpled paper and read the message written on it. Lavinia was less cautious than he; she had not attempted to disguise her writing, but there was no beginning and no end to her note.

'They have promised to dine at the Galtons' on Wednesday evening, and they will take Chrissie with them. I am also invited but I shall make an excuse to stay at home, at the last minute. Rose is almost certain to hear of this, but she will think I have gone too. It would be wiser to come here openly. In case the servants talk, you can invent some excuse, say you forgot they would all be out, and that you were worried about R. Thought her not so well, and wanted her mother to be sure to see her the next day. It will seem natural for you to stay a while and talk to me.'

Reluctantly, Ives tore the paper into small pieces and threw it on the fire. It was by no means a perfect plan, but what plan of this description could be? He could not believe that even if the meeting were discovered, anyone would think ill of them, for they had shown not the slightest interest in each other.

How easy to say that his very anxiety about Rose had led him to stay for some time talking of her to the sympathetic Lavinia. In any case whatever the risk he would take it, for by now there was such a bodily aching to see her and hold her again that it could not be denied.

In the hollow tree Lavinia must have found his answer. Only six words: '*By nine o'clock. Depend on me.*' There was little doubt but that she would.

CHAPTER 15

Later when the big entrance door opened and Lavinia came out as the doorbell pealed through the house, Ives stared at her in astonishment, but she put a finger to her lips, took his hand and drew him within.

'What about your horse and the trap?' she asked. 'Will they be all right there for an hour?'

'Yes – Maggie's a patient beast. Must it be only for an hour? What *is* all this, Lavinia? Why did you let me in? Is the house empty?'

'Almost. There's a servants' ball at Cheyney Grange. The housekeeper sent an invitation to all of them here, and Aunt Caroline said they could accept it. That was planned weeks ago, but nobody had thought to tell me about it. Mrs Cheyney arranged it for her butler and housekeeper who are man and wife and celebrating their silver wedding. They have been in her service for years. Aunt Caroline thought the four of us would be at the Galtons' place this evening. She was rather worried at leaving the three younger girls at home, and although she was sorry for me when I said I had raging neuralgia and couldn't possibly dine out, she was relieved too, as it would mean they were not alone. They're in bed and asleep, even Elsie. I looked in on them to be sure.'

'Then why only an hour?'

'Because it's long enough, Ives. The servants at the Dower House will probably know at what time you return, and it had better be fairly early. Millicent is a nervous child and has a trick of waking up about ten o'clock and coming downstairs. Generally, Miss Compton, the governess, is on the alert, but she is away on holiday. The only wise thing is for this visit to seem open and guileless. I shall tell Aunt Caroline about it tomorrow, and she will at once see Rose, who of course won't be told that you were worried about her, and drove over here to talk to her mother.'

Ives had followed Lavinia into the drawing-room. Instead of sitting down on the sofa where he could have been close to her, she took a winged, high-backed chair opposite.

'If we are to meet frequently in the future, how can it always seem guileless?' he asked.

'But it won't be known that we meet, or at least I hope not. If we are ever caught out, then we shall have to make it seem plausible. It's something we can't plan ahead; but there's a good deal that we *can* plan for the next few weeks. There are the light evenings, and Rose will rarely go beyond her own garden except for her daily drive. Each day when the workmen leave Pleasance there will be that great, empty, half-finished house. There is the park, the tangled gardens – who will notice us, even in the daytime? Nobody spies on you, Ives.'

'No – but what about you? Won't it be wondered where you are? My dear, of course it will.'

Lavinia smiled with calm confidence. She was wearing her white tea-gown in which she looked ethereal and remote. Although she was mapping out a treacherous scheme, she was in no mood to submit or to respond to lascivious caressing.

'I have my little music-room, and I spend hours there. By now the family are accustomed to it, and they don't disturb me. I have impressed on them that one interruption can spoil hours and hours of work.'

'Which would scarcely worry your aunt, who is thoroughly embarrassed over the nature of the songs that have brought you success.'

'I know, but lately Aunt Caroline and I have had several conversations about that. I've told her I intend to make a drastic change, and that in future I shall concentrate on ballads which reek of sweet sentiment. I even outlined one to her about a poor little crippled child whose one treasure is his pet canary, and the bird dies. It is vastly pathetic, believe me.'

'I do – though as there are several of such ballads now being sung by family sopranos, I doubt if your publisher or agent will be encouraging over that new departure.'

'I shan't solicit their encouragement. It won't be submitted to them. I shall compose the song as a means of reassuring Aunt Caroline, of making her sympathetic and well disposed to me. As it will be tedious work, it could be called, I suppose, a sacrifice.'

'To love?' Ives enquired softly.

'Is that the appropriate word?'

'Good God, Lavinia, haven't I been in love with you for years, and hasn't this miserable situation come about because when we were both free and you could have had me with honour, you wouldn't look at me?'

'If it is so miserable for you it need go no further,' she retorted coldly.

'It would be more miserable if it did not. Subterfuge will be distasteful to us both, but it would be unbearable not to have you – now. God knows where it will all end . . .'

'The end is too far away to worry us,' said Lavinia. 'Such affairs are common enough, and they rarely end tragically. Lovers tire, as married people tire of each other.'

'You speak from experience, no doubt.'

'Certainly I do. Joseph fell ill and died, but before he sickened I could scarcely endure to be in the same room with him, yet I had loved him with the extreme of passion . . .'

'Don't speak of him.' Abruptly Ives got up and knelt beside her. He put his arms round her slender waist. 'This, that you and I have is different. Tell me so. Was he satisfying to you as a lover?'

'Not satisfying at all, though I scarcely realized it. I was too inexperienced, and thought it natural to find the love act boring.'

'It isn't, you know, darling.'

'I do know – now. I knew that before Joe died.'

Who had taught her? he wondered jealously, but did not ask. She was not so aloof now, and she allowed him to kiss her. She even returned his kiss, but it was a poor thing when compared with the spontaneous embrace of weeks ago.

'You must go,' she said presently.

'But why? There's nobody about. Those children are all asleep.'

'I explained why. It's no good here – but it will be good in that empty house or in the park. We can't meet too often – but the first time can be soon. Choose a place and write to me . . .'

'Is it too far for you to walk?'

'I shall ride. I have my own horse now.'

'Lavinia, it's too risky. You will be seen. Young women don't ride unattended, especially in the evenings – not even in the summer evenings.'

'Then make our meetings earlier in the day, though you underrate all the work I have put in on Aunt Caroline. She thinks I am eccentric, but talented; that I must have freedom and not be bound by the rules that bind Rose and Chrissie. After all I am a widow, not a girl. She believes now that I shall become famous in a way that will be a credit to the entire family; though of course she still thinks that the ideal for any woman is to make a good marriage such as Rose has made.'

Suddenly and guiltily Ives's thoughts reverted to his young wife. 'Rose must never know of this,' he said.

'It would be a tremendous bore if she did – such scenes! Why do you worry so? It will be easy enough until this second child is born, and by then we may have tired of each other.'

'What you think, you cruel witch, is that you may have tired, as you tired of your husband. But I am no such weak, gambling fool.'

Lavinia threw back her head and laughed. His mouth came down savagely on her stretched throat and then she cried out half in fear, and half in pleasure. Her arms went round him and she strained him to her. She said : 'Rose might die having this child. Women do, often enough.'

'God forbid!' He was shocked back to sanity and got to his feet.

Unabashed, Lavinia said: 'If she did, you would marry me after a while, but I don't suppose she will die, and I don't want her to, poor fool; that's because I am only half-way in love with you as yet. Ives, when I was in Paris I heard a queer story about the Grenton family. Uncle Martin and the girls think they spring from the Grentons, don't they? Rose is said to be like that ancient ancestress, Annis Grenton.'

'She is. What do you know about the family?' Ives was momentarily diverted.

'A branch of the Pallistier family live in Paris, and amongst the many people I knew there, was one Pierre Pallistier. I told him I had an aunt who had married a Broughton and was descended from a Pallistier, and he was amused, for it seems there is a bar sinister. The long-ago ancestor who was given Pleasance by the artist Andrea Grenton, fathered a boy who was none of his, but was one of *Le Roi Soleil*'s bastards. He never knew – the child I mean, and it was his daughter who married a Broughton. Rose descends not from the English Grentons, but on the wrong side of the blanket from the King of France.'

Ives, who since acquiring Pleasance, had become absorbed in the history of the family, experienced an odd sense of shock. 'It may not be true,' he said. 'Nobody can vouch for such an ancient scandal.'

'But why invent it?' Lavinia divined that the story had disturbed him, and although she did not understand why, she was pleased. Having been badly hurt herself, it was a panacea to hurt others, even Ives who seemed under a compulsion to love her, and to whom she was now strongly attracted. She had said she was only half in love with him, but even that was too much to say. She wanted him, but love, she believed, was over for her. Love was trusting and tender. Lavinia was now incapable of tenderness; she had faith only in herself. When her husband had succumbed to drink and had gambled away her fortune, she had in her desperate misery surrendered to more than one man who was ready to help her with money or influence. Of those despairing months her relations knew nothing. As soon as her husband died, her mother had come to her aid. Her small income had been salvaged, and her step-father had helped her mother to pay Joseph Swan's debts. Lavinia herself had been treated as an invalid, though there had been little wrong with her. She had been cherished, yet had known that she was an embarrassment to her mother now remarried, and even more of an embarrassment because of the way in which she had exploited her musical talent. Cynical bitterness had never been greater than when meeting Ives again, she had discovered he was all she now desired.

Unjustly she blamed him. Why couldn't he have waited? He was older than she; he had loved her. He should have known that her marriage was bound to be a failure, and then he, not any of those others could have taken her, and on her wretched husband's death could have married her. Instead he had let her go, and he had married the rustic Rose, whose obvious charms must have appealed to him since nobody could take seriously the incident which was supposed to have compromised her.

Lavinia did not as yet thoroughly comprehend his obsession with Pleasance, now in process of resurrection. She supposed he was spending a fortune on it chiefly to please Rose who wished to live near her people.

'Isn't it rather fascinating to reflect that Rose and her sisters have royal blood in their veins?' she asked teasingly.

'I can't say that I find it so. But why in the world are we wasting time talking of long-past history? *Any* talk is a waste when we have only this snatched hour.'

'And the hour is over,' Lavinia reminded him, maddening in her seeming indifference.

He reached for her again, but as he did so there were footsteps heard outside the door, the handle turned and Millicent stood there in her nightshift, tousled-haired and eyes blinking sleepily.

'I woke up and I was hungry,' she whimpered.

'Well then, we must find you something to eat,' said Lavinia in a matter-of-fact voice. Her glance at Ives conveyed several things. Self-congratulation because she had decided there should be no secrecy about his visit, ironical amusement at his disappointment, and the injunction that he should leave now, without further delay.

Ives could only obey. As Lavinia, taking Millicent's hand, went down the long passage to the kitchen regions, he let himself out of the house, and drove home. It was still reasonably early, and he sent a servant for a groom to take the horse and trap round to the stables. Lavinia was right when she said it was better to avoid secrecy, though Rose would not know he had gone out after she was abed.

He smiled as it occurred to him that Lavinia had not thought to offer him any refreshment. That would have shocked her hospitable uncle and aunt, but perhaps her forgetfulness was a sight she was not so coolly mistress of herself as she had sought to impress upon him. He did not ring for the whisky which he now felt he needed but went into the dining-room and found, as he had expected, that the half-full decanter was still on the buffet. Filling his glass he looked round the room which was small compared with the dining-room now being constructed at Pleasance. Here, the walls were somewhat overcrowded with pictures, some of which he reflected would be the nucleus of a collection in the gallery at Pleasance. These would be few at the start, but they would be soon augmented. It was a pity there would be no portrait of Rose as she was at the time of their wedding. He was a fool not to have thought of it. He should have commissioned such a portrait from one of the modern fashionable painters. However she would look charming with the new baby in her arms, and little Esme leaning against her knee. He, Ives supposed, had better be painted in riding kit, in which he knew that he looked well. A pity it would be impossible to include in their collection the lovely Lavinia in her white tea-gown.

Across the room and almost level with his eyes was the plump and comely face of Annis Grenton. Because of Rose's resemblance to this picture the Squire had given it to her as an additional wedding present, unaware that he had been prompted to this generosity by hints from Ives, for it was he not Rose who coveted Annis's portrait.

Glass in hand, he walked across the room to examine it more closely. There was so much life in it that the unknown artist must have had some talent, and it seemed certain that it had been a good likeness of this early Grenton whom Chrissie, odd girl that she was, considered sinister. Now comparing the pictured face with Rose's living face, he was forced to own that the reputed likeness had nothing to do with features, and was merely one of colouring and plumpness.

Could there be anything in Lavinia's story of a bar sinister; of the French King's bastard who had been fathered by Jacques Pallistier? He had come upon nothing in the family records which had echoed that old scandal; but one of the treasures saved from Pleasance at the time of the fire had been an ancient ivory rattle, reputed to have been a present from Louis to Jacques's wife, Eloise, when she was expecting the child whose birth had been partially responsible for her death.

It was absurd that long after the Grenton and Pallistier name had become amalgamated with the Broughtons this should seem of any account, and yet it was of account to him for it had pleased him to think of that long line which would be continued through his children. Some of the charm Rose still had for him seemed to have evaporated.

Not that anyone aware of his secret passion for her cousin Lavinia would believe he cared for Rose. He pondered, for once able to take a detached view of Lavinia. How much was he prepared to sacrifice for her? Undoubtedly this secret love would entail sacrifices.

He could, of course, set her up in a home of her own, in London preferably, and it should not be difficult to deceive her mother and aunt and cousins. They could be told and would not question it, that through the money acquired by her musical compositions she could afford an establishment of her own. The devil of it was that Pleasance was too far from London to make it easy to see her frequently. He would have to invent reasons for visiting London, and could think of none that would seem plausible. Moreover, Rose would expect to accompany him. The best solution would be to give her plenty of children which would keep her tethered here. But as that callous thought passed across his mind Ives, who was not callous by nature, experienced a softening, a surge of compassion. Poor Rose, trying hard now to be patient and uncomplaining over this second pregnancy. She deserved some gaiety, poor child, and he would not grudge it to her, but it was a pity she could enjoy nothing unless he was her companion. Less devoted to him and she could go on a European trip with a suitable duenna, and Chrissie as her companion. The babies could be left to their nurse.

But that was a scheme to which Rose would never agree, though it might have solved his problem over Lavinia, for who could then have raised a protest had he absented himself for weeks?

Absented himself from Pleasance! The cold, stunning truth suddenly struck him. He wouldn't want to. Not even to be with Lavinia would he for long desert the house and the estate, upon the planning of which he had expended so much creative zeal. Pleasance and Lavinia were in competition, and for the life of him he could not have said which of the two meant the more to him.

❋ CHAPTER 16 ❋

Less than a fortnight later the lovers met and were alone. It was a Sunday, and there was no foreseeable danger of discovery. At Derevale, Caroline was absent, but that was because she was taking her Sunday school class in the village, a pious task which only severe illness would have made her shirk. The Squire was having his usual Sunday nap. The younger girls had gone for a country walk with their governess. Christobel was with Rose who had been recommended by her doctor to take carriage airing each day. Rose did not cavil at that, but was inclined to be peevish because Ives could rarely if ever accompany her. Christobel was a poor substitute. Owen was spending the week-end with his family in Lincoln.

Lavinia rode over on horseback. It was impossible on a sunny afternoon to do that other than openly, though she had not announced her intention to the family who supposed, if they gave a thought to her, that she was shut away in her own room.

Although Caroline was conventionally strict over religious observances and Sunday was a day set apart, she could not think it wrong for her niece to be occupied with her music, for just lately Lavinia had given forth that she had started work on a song cycle which would be of a strictly religious nature. Caroline was delighted, taking this as a result of the long talks she had had with her niece on the duty of worthily using a natural gift. Letters about that were now exchanged with Lavinia's mother who wrote that she was deeply grateful to her elder sister. The horrid French songs would be forgotten in time and they would all be proud of Lavinia, who had changed so satisfactorily under Caroline's influence.

'I did not meet a soul I knew on the way,' said Lavinia, as Ives helped her to dismount from her horse. 'There is hardly anyone about. What a dead place this is on a Sunday afternoon. How in the world do people occupy themselves?'

'In the case of lovers it might be imprudent to ask,' Ives said smiling, 'but the older people who work hard for six days a week, and on a Sunday eat a hearty midday meal, are slumbering heavily behind drawn blinds.'

Lavinia had seen Pleasance several times before, but today it looked different to her, and while Ives took her horse round to the stables, she gazed at it consideringly.

Much progress had been made since she was last here. The fine May weather must have helped. Part of the roof was on, and as that was composed of silver-coloured tiles it was very striking. Most of the window apertures were as yet devoid of glass panes, but the few that there were glittered in the sunshine. The house, which would be magnificent when completed, already looked pleased with itself, thought Lavinia. Why did it remind her of something feline: an enormous, drowsy cat perhaps?

Ives returned to her and took her arm, leading her around the east side of the house, and then smiled at her surprise, for here there was a small, outjutting wing, no more than a chalet, and all on one floor. It was roofed and windowed. Lavinia noticed at once that the stone walls were old, reminding her of some ancient Norman tower; the slabs were of different shapes and sizes, but all fitted snugly into one another. There was a tall, metal door, of iron probably. The low roof was eaved; the windows were of an oriel shape.

'Well, what do you think of it?' Ives asked.

'It's an anachronism.'

'Those walls, if they could speak, would say the remainder of the house is that. This wing, if it can be called a wing, has been salvaged from the old Pleasance. The foundations are new, for there was no such annex when the last of the Pallistiers lived here, but stone by stone the old walls were built up again, and the door was one which originally locked off the cellars. The roof and windows are new, of course. It may not be exactly beautiful, but it can't be seen from the main frontage, and it pleases me.'

'You gratified a whim, Ives, not caring whether it was appropriate or whether it was not.'.

'Exactly. I wanted a small place which would be entirely my own. I call it my office, and here I shall conduct all the business connected with the estate.'

'Will there be a great deal?'

'It will grow. I have a fancy to breed horses as the Grentons did in the Tudor days. That necessitates stableboys, grooms, trainers. Then, too, there will be the home farm . . .' He broke off and said: 'But you're not here to listen to my schemes for the future.'

'Not today, though they may be of importance to me.'

Ives did not ask her what she meant. He sensed that she already thought of Pleasance as a rival, and so it was. He wished it could be otherwise, but it would be Rose who would share that side of his life, if any woman *could* share it. He took a large and clumsy key from his pocket and unlocked the door saying: 'We shall be safe here, for today at least. Rose already calls it my Bluebeard's Chamber, for I told her that when here I wished to be private. All the rest of the house will be hers, and within reason she can do as she chooses with it, but this small part of it is mine alone.'

'And you think I shall come to you here by stealth?' Lavinia enquired with disdain.

'Occasionally perhaps, when there are none to notice.'

The old massive door was opened, but Lavinia felt reluctant to cross the threshold. She hung back, and Ives entered before her and drew her in. Although the room was fully furnished and the sun shone through the windows, she shivered as though with cold. Ives was smiling at her with delight, yet she felt unwanted; there was no welcome for her here. That sensation was so strong and so unpleasant that it muffled natural curiosity as she glanced round the room which was long and low, with heavy oak beams supporting the ceiling. The stone walls were covered with tapestry panels; there were heavy curtains to draw across the windows; a thick carpet covered the floor. Shelves were as yet empty of books, the desk was bare, but a wide sofa which was more like a bed was furnished with cushions and rugs.

'You have made it very comfortable,' said Lavinia, herself feeling far from comfortable.

But if there was a hostile element Ives was evidently unaffected by it, and perhaps it was not hostile to him, who gave devotion and service to the new creation formed on the ruins of the old. It would get neither from her, thought Lavinia resentfully. If the passion that had flared up between them was to be more than an interlude, she would fight this house, prise him away from it and take him wholly for herself. The thought revitalized her and she turned herself to him.

'Sometimes when I am working late, I may sleep here, rather than disturb Rose,' he said.

Lavinia was not jealous of Rose. She was confident that when the time came, if she wanted him enough, she could displace her cousin. But to supplant the house he had built would be harder.

Ives pulled off her leather gloves. He looked at her questioningly, and then as she raised her arms to take off her hard-brimmed riding-hat, he went to the window to draw the curtains. Lavinia threw the hat upon the sofa. It had flattened the coils of her *blonde-cendre* hair, giving her a childish look, and Ives thought there was shyness in her lop-sided smile. He wanted to think so, as he drew her to him and started to unbutton the bodice of her tight habit. There were at least a dozen buttons, and Lavinia smiled down at his awkward fingers.

❋ CHAPTER 17 ❋

Christobel had always had a secret world of her own, jealously preserved and sweet to her. It was an entirely innocent world, alive with the thoughts that nobody else could be expected to understand, and with the memory of events which would have seemed unremarkable to everyone except herself.

There were remembered sensations; the wonder which had struck her when she had walked through a wood, with the boughs of the trees so tightly laced above her that although it was raining heavily she had only known it because of the pattering noise and the shivering of the leaves. There was the burning fatigue of one overlong dusty walk and the exquisite pleasure of the cool bath when she reached home. There was a moment of extreme happiness when she had rescued a young starling from the cruel mouth of one of the stable cats and had realized that the bird was almost unhurt and was not afraid of her. She had smoothed its feathers and it had rested in her hands, and when it had flown away it was not because it was suddenly afraid, but because it had recovered its strength.

The occasions when she had known fear, and the helplessness which all children experience from time to time were shut away and rarely examined. Above all she remembered first meeting Owen, remembered his smiling eyes and the conviction that had come upon her, that they were not strangers. She had thought then and many times since that there was nothing in the world she couldn't tell him, and that if she ever let him into her secret world he would know why it was important to her. Yet here she was sitting on one of the broad stone window-seats in the banqueting hall at Pleasance, where the vaulted ceiling was no longer open to the sky, wondering if she ever could tell him about this new, horrible worry; wondering if she ought to tell him; wondering if he could be of any help if she did.

The minstrels' gallery had yet to be painted, and might not be considered satisfactory in its present state, for Owen was doubtful, though Ives was content. As now constructed it lacked importance, Owen said. It should be wider, deeper, and have more of the appearance of a flying buttress. He was despondent because a good deal of money had been spent to such poor effect, and the fault was his, since he was the designer.

Ives made light of it. The work on the gallery was not finished and it could be demolished. If Owen was dissatisfied he could start all over again. Expense was unimportant. A fact which appeared to unduly depress Owen.

Later, Ives left him alone in the great hall with Christobel. More than ever now he had a kindly feeling for lovers. He had promised, he said, to take Rose for a perambulation round the grounds. She had arrived at the stage when she disliked moving more than a few yards from the Dower House, being exaggeratedly conscious of her clumsiness and afraid that she might fall. One was always being told, Ives remarked cheerfully, that to have children was a natural process for a woman, but according to his experience it was a long drawn-out illness.

Owen sat down by Christobel on the window-seat and said: 'He's the most open-handed, generous fellow. If a new gallery is made it will cost a mint of money.'

'He can afford it,' said Christobel.

'It's the thought of that – the being aware that he can squander so much and scarcely know it, that I find depressing. A fortune has been spent already on this place, and only for his own gratification.'

Rather surprised, Christobel said: 'But that's always the case when a great, new house is built, and Pleasance will now descend to many generations. As for the building of it, isn't that giving work to many who need work?'

'Including myself – yes, it is. I should be the last to carp because expenditure is of little account to Ives. I did not give a great deal of thought to it, until I was at home these last few days. My sister was also at home and she was in an anxious state.'

'The one who is a nun?'

'Her community call themselves a sisterhood. They have not taken life-long vows, though it would be hard to imagine Eliza breaking hers. They have their settlement in a poor quarter, and they have been given notice to quit. The owner, who is a grasping rogue, intends to let it out in tenement dwellings which will greatly augment his revenue. The Sisterhood are not wealthy, and they can pay no more in rent than they pay at present. Moreover, they have already spent much from their private funds on repairs. It is a barracks of a place and in a tumbledown condition, not really suitable for their purpose, but they can find no other, and they cannot afford to build.'

'Then what will happen, Owen?'

'Presumably they will be forced to disband, hope to find a place for their orphan girls in other such homes, and hope to find themselves needed elsewhere. Eliza is deeply grieved for she has done so much good and loves all the children under her care. They are devoted to her. It is delightful to see her with them. Now the work of the last ten years will go for nought. Eliza is in her middle thirties and she has given her youth to it.'

It was unnecessary for Christobel to express her sympathy in words. Her expression was eloquent as she pressed his hand. She said after a pause: 'Your sister must be a wonderful person – a saint.'

Owen smiled at that. 'If so, she is a very human saint. She has a great sense of fun; she is impulsive and not without vanity. As an example, she detests her name of Eliza and much prefers to be known as Sister Monica, which is her religious name.'

'She sounds as though she would be very nice to know. I do hope she gets help and can start up the settlement elsewhere. It is not only a children's orphanage is it?'

'No. It's also a convalescent home for mothers in need of rest and care. Both before and after birth they can take refuge there. Eliza has nursing experience and so have several of her colleagues. It is too early to despair. They have a few weeks' grace, and there are many good people who with voluntary gifts have kept this place going. One may come forward and offer to help.'

'I wonder if Ives would.'

Owen shook his head. 'I could not suggest it. He has already done too much for me. My salary is more than liberal. Our family might find some of the capital needed, I dare say, but not enough.'

'It would do Ives much more good to expend money on a Cause than on starting stables for racing horses and for breeding them,' said Christobel. 'Rose says that is his intention as soon as Pleasance is finished and they are living here. He could lose a fortune on it.'

'Or more probably make one. He is a shrewd fellow, for all his careless generosity.'

'Oh, why should generosity count for so much? Why should he be popular because he has a pleasant way with him? He has everything in the world he wants.' Christobel spoke with a force that surprised Owen.

'I know you have never wholly liked him,' he said, 'but you sounded then as though you hated him.'

'I think I do,' said Christobel in a low voice.

'Why do you, my love?'

She sighed, looking down at his fingers that were closed around hers and said: 'Perhaps I should keep it to myself, but I must tell somebody, and there is no one else I can trust.'

'Then tell me, my darling.'

'Ives is having a love affair with Lavinia.'

There was a moment of startled silence before Owen said: 'You wouldn't make such an accusation unless you were sure, but how can you be sure? When have they had the opportunity to be together?'

'I dare say they have contrived different times. I did not suspect they took any interest in each other, and I'm sure Rose does not, though she knows Ives was in love with Lavinia before she married Joseph Swan. Poor Rose – she loves him and trusts him and he's always kind to her, though I've never thought he was wildly in love with her. But Rose was satisfied, and ever since Livvy came here to stay, she has underrated her. She says she has lost her beauty and looks older than her age; but I think there are times when she is very beautiful, and she is fascinating, Owen. She fascinated me, at first.'

'Only at first?'

'Yes, for after a while I pitied her. I seemed to realize she was false all through, and that what had once been good in her, had been burnt out by bitterness. She has been badly treated and it has made her cruel. I expect that even her love for Ives is half cruelty. She was with him here on Sunday. I was driving with Rose, but after a very short while the bumping on the roads made her feel sick, and she told Grenge to drive us home. She went to lie down, and didn't want me – so I came over here – I don't know why, because as a rule I hate being at Pleasance, hate being in the grounds by myself. I saw the curtains drawn in the small wing at the back which Ives says is to be for himself alone. But a fold of one curtain was hitched aside, and I could see the back of a chair, with Lavinia's green habit thrown across it. Then I heard a voice – I couldn't hear the words, but it was Ives's voice . . . I went quickly away.'

'You could have been mistaken,' said Owen.

'In the voice? Yes, I could, though I know Ives has the key and he wouldn't give it to anyone else. But I couldn't make a mistake about the habit. Only Lavinia has a green cloth one. It has mother-of-pearl buttons and I recognized them as well.'

'But even if she were there with Ives, there could have been some reason – '

'For undressing?' Christobel in her scorn ignored all inhibiting delicacy. 'A riding habit is not like an ordinary coat with a dress beneath it. One wears only one's underclothes.

'Oh, Owen, I've been so unhappy. What can I do?'

'Nothing. You can only try to forget it.'

'How can I? When I am with Livvy I feel I hate her, and to me she looks different. More beautiful, but in a frightening kind of way . . . smooth and cruel, and amused by poor Rose who is now such a dreadful shape, and moans so about herself. I watched Livvy only yesterday when they were together. She was talking to Rose in a purring soft voice, saying it would soon be over, and how proud Ives would be of her . . . but there was a sneer in it.'

'Oh, God, I wish you knew nothing about it. My poor sweet, you are far too young to manage such a situation. But if your mother were to be told . . .'

'Oh, no, no!' Christobel was horrified. 'Poor Mama, it would nearly kill her, and she wouldn't know what to do, except to send Lavinia back to Aunt Hilda, which wouldn't be the least bit of good.'

'Wouldn't it? At least she would be miles away from here.'

'She might not be. Nobody could force Lavinia to return to Aunt Hilda. She has money of her own and Ives would give her more; all she wanted. He might even want to join her.'

Owen shook his head. 'I don't believe he would. Pleasance means too much to him.'

'Perhaps by now Ives means too much to Pleasance. It's such a living thing – not just bricks and mortar as it ought to be. At first the – the forces that control Pleasance may have been doubtful about the upheaval which Ives planned to bring about, but by now as he's so dedicated . . . well, he won't be allowed to go, not easily. Ghosts, spirits, shades . . . I'm not sure what they are, but they'll fight.'

Christobel had relaxed and spoke dreamily. She was giving voice to what she believed, what she had believed even as a child.

'That's only another way of saying that most old places have their spell,' said Owen.

'So it is, and I dare say such a spell can be either benevolent or malignant. I don't know if Pleasance is malignant – now. It was at first I imagine, when there were those accidents. It had become used to its peace and neglect, but thanks to you it's becoming a beautiful place, so why shouldn't it be appreciative? The grounds, especially the park are different. Ives is destroying too much. That's bound to be resented.'

Throughout the course of months, Owen had become so used to her fantasies that he could accept them. He said: 'I'm glad that when we are married we shan't live here. I'm looking forward to having a bright, happy, loving wife, not one who is caught up in a dream-trance. I'll build a modern house for you, my love, and *we* will make its history.'

'That will be nice,' said Christobel contentedly. 'I wish it could be soon.'

'Oh, lord, so do I . . . it's not good for you, all this, feeling as though you are part of a haunted landscape. And now you have to discover an intrigue. I still think your mother should know about it, or perhaps the Squire . . .'

'I couldn't possibly tell either of them,' said Christobel firmly, 'not until Rose's baby is born. Mama would think herself capable of hiding it, but Rose can be shrewd, and she knows Mama so well. She would guess from her manner that something was wrong, and she would probe and probe until she found out. Then when she did, the shock of it would be terrible. It might do her an injury – the baby as well.'

'It might indeed.' Owen groaned. 'The only thing is to do nothing – at least for the present.'

She said doubtfully: 'I might speak to Lavinia . . .'

'My love, she would only deny it. She would say you had been dreaming; she might even be able to prove to you that she was a long way from Pleasance last Sunday afternoon.'

'She *could* prove it,' cried Christobel, suddenly remembering. 'She said at luncheon that she was going to do some work on her song cycle, and would then ride over to see the Merriless girls at Willow Hall. This morning I met Eva Merriless, and she said how much they had enjoyed having Livvy there, and that she had made several suggestions about Eva's trousseau. She is getting married in the early autumn to Captain Roth. I suppose Livvy could have got from here to Willow Hall, it's not so very far away, but it would have been quite an undertaking. Owen, do you think it was imagination? I saw that riding habit so clearly. Is it possible I was seeing something that was going to happen – a kind of prescience? But what would be the good of it?'

'I don't think anything of the kind.' He knew that Christobel was terrified of the supernatural when she was involved in it. 'Your cousin thinks nothing of lashing her horse to a lather, in order to get the last ounce of speed out of the poor beast. I've seen her tearing across the countryside. No doubt she did ride over to Willow Hall. You weren't told when she arrived – whether it was late or early?'

'No – I was in a dream as usual, and did not even remember until just now that it was the same afternoon. Oh, what's the good of having told you? I hoped you would know what to do.'

For the first time since they had met, and with a dazzling certainty known there was a link between them, she was gazing at him with disappointment, as though he had failed her. Owen said: 'Darling, I've told you what I think should be done, but you have put up objections, and they're sound enough. It might be better not to interfere, to allow the affair to blow over.'

Christobel could not imagine that such a love affair would, or at least not easily. Young and inexperienced though she was, she did not under-assess Lavinia's attraction. On first meeting her, Christobel had been reminded of a heroine in a romantic novel; but there were not only heroines in novels, there were ruthless sirens. Lavinia, she thought, was a very special kind of siren, one who would want to hurt even if she loved. When Ives had first known her and wanted to marry her, she had been a spoilt, arrogant girl, who could not imagine that anyone would ever treat her badly. She had learnt differently, and it had set up a poison in her. Now she might look much the same as the Lavinia of two years ago, but she was very different.

'It won't matter to Livvy if she breaks up Rose's world and makes us all dreadfully miserable,' began Christobel, but then the words broke off sharply, for she realized they had been overheard. She had forgotten the open window, and Ives had crossed on the soft turf.

Owen got up, and Christobel shrank back in a corner of the stone seat as Ives put a long leg over the sill, and climbed in. He looked from one to the other with curiosity. 'Sorry, but I couldn't help hearing what you said, Chrissie. Something about Lavinia making you all miserable and not caring if she did. What is it all about?'

Christobel looked at him beseechingly. She said: 'Oh, Ives, I wish I had imagined it, but I know I didn't.' Tears shone in her eyes, and suddenly she was a little girl again.

Although Ives did not particularly care for Christobel –

with her beautiful but dreamy eyes, the something fey and ethereal about her which to him was an irritation – she was so piteous and so devoid of her usual aloof young dignity that he softened to her. 'Tell me all about it,' he invited. 'No, don't stop her, Owen.'

'Since it has got so far, I can tell you myself,' said Owen, putting an arm around Christobel. 'If I do, it may upset her less. She has the idea that you and Lavinia were shut away here together last Sunday afternoon. Rose cut their drive short, it seems; she felt ill and came home. Chrissie left her resting and wandered over here. The curtains were drawn, but part of one was pulled aside, and she saw Lavinia's green riding habit draped over the back of a chair near the window. She thought, too, that she heard your voice, but she wasn't sure . . .'

'And came to the obvious conclusion, no doubt,' said Ives who had listened attentively and with perfect calm, 'though for a well brought-up young lady, Chrissie, you ought to have been blankly mystified, instead of adroitly putting two and two together.'

'I wish I had been blankly mystified.' Christobel gulped down a childish sob.

Ives smiled at her kindly: 'Never mind, my dear, I am glad I overheard you, for now I can set your mind at rest. Lavinia *was* here. Riding over the fields, I saw her in the distance, or rather I saw her horse. She had taken a toss and was on the ground. She wasn't hurt, but she was shaken and also extremely angry. You know how she prides herself on her horsemanship, but something or other had scared the animal, and he had bolted, and had thrown her out of the saddle. I captured the horse and made Lavinia mount again; the best thing to do if anyone has been thrown, but is uninjured. She was shaken, as I say, but she could keep her seat and I brought her along to the office wing, which alone is furnished. It is nearer than the Dower House, besides which I wasn't sure if Rose was there or not, and wouldn't run the risk of alarming her by letting her see Lavinia so shaken and dishevelled. Her habit was muddy, and I told her to take it off so that I could brush it. I had a cloak of my own here, which I've put on sometimes when I was working late and it has turned cold. I wrapped it round her, gave her some brandy from my flask; not much, but sufficient to steady her. Naturally I pulled the blinds in case anyone passed the windows. I made her lie down on the sofa wrapped in my cloak, and I took her habit into the adjoining pantry, where there is running water. I sponged the coat and skirt and made them look presentable. When I returned Livvy had dozed off – due to the brandy, I dare say. I put the habit on a chair and let her sleep for a while, and then I roused her. She seemed quite herself and insisted on riding over to Willow Hall as she had arranged – some business with Eva Merriless about a trousseau, she told me. Lavinia can be very stubborn, and nothing would induce her to let me drive her back to Derevale. She made me promise to say nothing to your mother, because of the fuss there might be. I rode with her until we were within sight of Willow Hall, and then because she insisted, I left her. That is what happened and I admit I considered it sensible to keep quiet about it. Not only because your mother might be in a fume over the accident, but because she might think the incident a compromising one. Not until I came to England did I realize how excessively easy it is to compromise a girl. Now are you satisfied?'

Christobel had listened, not taking her eyes from his face. She said: 'I'm sorry, Ives. Owen said there must be an explanation. Why did I have to believe what was horrible?'

'One should always ask for an explanation before coming to a conclusion,' said Ives in quiet reproof.

Christobel accepted that meekly, and was as much rebuked by Owen's relief. She had spoilt one of their rare and precious hours. Ives went on to say that if Christobel wished she could question Lavinia, who would of course tell her exactly what he had told her. Christobel shook her head with an expression of distaste.

'Oh no! I want to forget it. I shall never speak of it again.'

Ives hoped she wouldn't have second thoughts about it. When she said she would walk over to the Dower House, Owen went with her, and Ives watched them moodily from the window. He had never thought of himself as a fluent liar and could not explain how, when taken by surprise, the plausible story of an accident had instantly occurred to him.

Although he congratulated himself, he was also ashamed. It would be as well to warn Lavinia in case Christobel said something that puzzled her, for then she might inadvertently betray herself. As it was, Christobel had made it difficult for them to meet again at Pleasance, or anywhere else for that matter, he reflected gloomily. She would not be so easily reassured a second time were she to see them together. Fortunately Lavinia searched every day in their secret post-office for a letter from him, and she would receive one on the morrow.

Restless, hating the mesh of deceit in which he was now caught, half-wishing that he had the strength of will to put Lavinia out of his life, but at the same time passionately craving for her, Ives went off to the park where the trees which for many years had been left undisturbed were being thinned out. A temporary shed had been put up in a clearing and here the tools and hand-trucks used by the woodmen, who from time to time gave him assistance, were kept.

Although in this part of the world, the trade of woodcutter was a dying one, Ives could have contracted with men from a different part of the country. That he did not do so was not for purposes of economy, but because there was no particular hurry to bring the park into order, and there was a primitive pleasure in doing much of the work himself. He had great bodily strength and was proud of his powerful arms that could wield an axe with such good effect. The heavy, manual work did something to assuage his restlessness; but today having written his warning letter to Lavinia, he was for the first time conscious of what Christobel would have called a resentful atmosphere. Ives did not so describe it, but strove to shake off a heaviness which he attributed to the airless day. Yet beyond the park the sun was shining, and there was a pleasant breeze. It was not really extraordinary, thought Ives, that one should have the sensation of the trees pressing in upon one. Their density gave a sense of imprisonment, and it was odd that although there must be many nesting birds in the thick branches, he had rarely heard them sing.

Glancing up he could see only leaves and branches, not a trace of the blue sky, though already several trees had been felled and would be sold for timber. Although in winter, huge wood fires would one day blaze in the grates at Pleasance, they would require only a fraction of what the park would yield when it was cleared.

There was one tree in particular for which Ives felt a positive dislike. It was an oak of enormous height and girth, and by some clasically minded owner of Pleasance had been christened The Hydra. Ives suspected that Nicholas, Annis Grenton's husband, who was a Greek scholar, might have devised this name; and it was appropriate, for the branches spread out in at least seven directions, and although lately many of these had been lopped off, the foliage was still dense. Smaller trees had been felled, so that now the giant towered in a cleared area.

He would do away with it altogether, Ives decided. He would saw through the trunk by degrees, though that would take days if he tackled it without aid. But he could make a start on it, and with a certain savage satisfaction as though about to smite an enemy to the ground, he raised the axe and struck. Although all his force was behind the blow, he barely grazed the massive trunk, but a second blow caused a perceptible fissure and the branches trembled. Ives laughed aloud, almost as though he had successfully attacked a human foe.

'Your days are numbered,' he triumphed, and it seemed as though all around him there was a listening silence.

CHAPTER 18

'But if you think,' said Lavinia in a sweet, cool voice, 'that I will submit to this treatment you must be exceedingly foolish. Tell me one good reason why I should.'

In full view of those within the drawing-room at Derevale Manor, she paced the terrace with Ives. There had been a family dinner-party to celebrate the Squire's birthday, and he now sat in the centre of a group looking well-pleased with himself, replete with good fare, and the more benign because for the occasion half-a-dozen bottles of a fine wine, laid down by his father years ago, had been brought up from the cellar.

The women of the family had elegantly sipped a glass apiece. Ives and Owen who had been invited took somewhat more; the Squire was far from abstemious. Caroline, worried by his flushed face, glittering eyes and heavy breathing, dispensed black coffee in the drawing-room. She had begged Ives in a whisper to see that her husband did not linger long after she and her daughters and niece had left them to their port and cigars.

Even Adelaide had been permitted to appear at dinner for the birthday celebration at which the Squire's health was ceremoniously toasted, but she and Millicent had been hustled off to bed by their governess before the gentlemen rejoined the remainder of the family.

Presents had been bestowed which caused the Squire to wipe away a sentimental tear. All their own work, Caroline had announced with pride, and the Squire at once slid his spectacles into the embroidered case that Millicent had made, and declared that the elaborate braces and slippers which were Elsie's and Christobel's handiwork were almost too magnificent for ordinary use. They should be treasured as heirlooms he said jestingly. Rose had knitted him a silk scarf which was by no means faultless but Lavinia, to everyone's surprise, had ordered a new saddle for his favourite roan, an expensive gift which the Squire much appreciated.

'A generous girl upon my word, as well as a good-looker,' he said as he was coaxed to drink his second cup of black coffee. 'Livvy is much improved from the days when she looked like a drooping lily. M'dear, we ought to bestir ourselves and find a second husband for her. There's more than one prospect living within fifty miles.'

'I have thought the same, Papa,' said Rose. 'Livvy is no longer in mourning and one can entertain for her. I'm determined to do my best once I've presented Ives with his son and heir.'

'That calls for another toast, m'dear . . .'

'In coffee,' said Caroline firmly. 'Remember those twinges of gout recently and Dr Sayle's warnings.'

The Squire grumbled that the family physician was a

milksop and an old woman, but being fearful when he recalled the solemn warnings, he did not demand brandy in his coffee. Christobel was playing softly at the piano, and Owen stood beside her to turn the pages of her music. Lavinia presently murmured that the night was very warm, and Ives held open the long window for her, and stepped out after her.

'Keep within their sight, and Rose will feel nothing but benevolence,' Lavinia murmured, 'and see that your voice is low. Who will then imagine that we are rending each other with savage words?'

'All the rending is on your side,' Ives returned. 'The complications must be perfectly clear to you, and it cannot be your wish any more than it is mine to cause distress and scandal.'

'Oh, as for that, I care little, so long as I am not here to see it. Once we are away they can all indulge in gnashing of teeth and wringing of hands. What will it then matter to me? Remember, I have already eloped once, and it was conducted with the utmost success and without the slightest suspicion. That I am prepared to do again, as I have told you, but not to stay on here in this dull place for week after week, seeing you alone only at rare intervals, and then but for a few minutes. It's a poor compliment to me that you can endure it with such fortitude.'

'Only outward fortitude,' said Ives. 'If you could have any idea of the sense of deprivation, the frustration . . .'

Turning her head she glanced at him, a slow, provocative glance from beneath her lowered lids. 'Then end the frustration,' she advised. 'It is not I who hang back. I am prepared to throw aside all else and to live abroad with you; to marry you if Rose gets a divorce; to be your mistress if she refuses. Is not that proof of my love?'

'I should be glad to think so.'

'But how can you think anything else?'

'Lavinia – ' he began, but she checked him with a small, swift gesture.

'Not so loudly, and don't turn to me in that expressive way. Your manner is as eloquent as clearly heard words. Now as we pass the full light from the window, make a beckoning gesture to Elsie. If she joins us it will be a pity, but it's unlikely she'll tear herself away from that tray of sugared fruits.' A moment later, Lavinia smiled: 'I told you so. Why should the child want to walk with a dull, grown-up brother-in-law and a widowed cousin, when she can sit there and gorge herself? She and Rose are both like their father, over-indulgent to their stomachs.'

'How you despise and dislike Rose. What harm has she ever done to you?'

'Didn't she take you from me?'

'No. I was at that time the least wanted person in your life.'

Lavinia sighed, and turned her eyes upon him with a wounded look. 'Since you already loved me, you should have waited for me. You might have known that soon, very soon I should be in need of you.'

'I did not so flatter myself, nor did I know that the man you preferred was of such poor quality. I had barely exchanged a word with him.'

'It's true I was very foolish,' said Lavinia with unfamiliar meekness, 'but I had little experience and he had romantic looks and a pretty turn of speech. It was your fault that I did not like you, for you had a curt, domineering manner and seemed to pride yourself on being an American.'

'I still do, though like most of my compatriots I have a sentimental weakness for the old country. My dream as a boy was to settle here. Pleasance was the house I wanted, though I had no expectation of ever getting it.'

'But I,' she murmured beguilingly, 'am I not more to you than any house?'

Was she, or was she not? Ives found it impossible to decide, and saw no reason why he should be called upon to make such a choice. He could keep Pleasance and also keep Lavinia, if only in the background of his life. Anger at her obstinacy hardened his voice as he said: 'You rate yourself high, m'dear. Am I to surrender not only my estate, but also my wife and daughter, and as like as not a son soon to be born?'

'Do I not also surrender something? My good name, my mother, all my relations? Pleasance is an obsession with you, always has been, from your childhood when you were first told about it. But it is I, not Rose, who can be the wife of your dreams, and I, too, can give you children.'

'That remains to be proved.' But at the thought of Lavinia with his babe in her arms, Ives's heart thundered, and he desired her madly.

'You need have no fear,' she said coolly. 'I shall breed for you. For Joseph I would not. I was with child some months after our marriage, but by then I was well aware of what he was, and I did not want the babe. There are ways and means . . . and the child within me perished.'

'For pity's sake! Had you no care for yourself? You could have been injured.'

Lavinia shook her head with a smile. 'I came to no harm. It was at the start of pregnancy. Afterwards I was assured by a physician in Paris that all was well with me – that I was strong and fertile.'

Ives could believe her. She was lithe for all her air of fragility. She was beautifully made. It was the plump women such as Rose who, oddly enough to his thinking, carried their unborn children with pain and sickness, and were in danger when their time came.

'Why should I not rate myself high?' Lavinia asked, and for an instant as they were at the end of the terrace and out of sight of the drawing-room window, she brushed nearer to him. It was as much as he could do not to seize her, and knowing that, she laughed at him. 'Well, think it over,' she challenged. 'But remember, I will never be hidden away in some London love nest. If I transgress, then I do so openly. When Rose understands that you will not return, she will rid herself of you, and in Italy or France you can build a house as beautiful as Pleasance.'

'It's impossible to make such a choice in haste,' said Ives.

'You have until Rose's child is safely born.'

'You care nothing for her safety. You once hinted your hope that she will die in childbed.'

Lavinia shrugged. 'It would,' she said, 'simplify the future, but given the choice I prefer her to live. If she died, your remorse would be excessive, and I should still have to separate you from Pleasance. I know that will be difficult, but be sure,

Ives, that I will never live there. Although I am no visionary, there are times when I am conscious of a menace. There is also your love for the place, which could become greater than your love for any woman, even for me.'

'Now you are rating yourself too low,' said Ives, aware of his possible insincerity.

'Far from it.' Lavinia's smile was suddenly sweet and mischievous. 'For I am convinced I shall be worth all you lose. It will be better if you decide without being influenced by my presence here. I shall leave next week, before the baby is born. You have a free choice, my love. Stay with Rose, see your son if she gives you a son, give your time to Pleasance, and if you discover that I mean more to you than all else, then you will come to me, and it will be for our happiness.'

Ives could not answer her, for as she ceased to speak they were once again crossing the track of the lighted windows, and Elsie jumped up and ran across the room to them.

'Now I shall walk with you,' she said beamingly, sure of her welcome, 'for there are only two dates left, stuffed with marzipan, and marzipan makes me feel sick.'

She edged herself between them, and took Ives's arm, looking up at him coquettishly, as she fancied she had seen Rose look when they thus walked together.

Lavinia was scarcely aware of the child's affectations. She had made her challenge and now wondered if she had been too bold, too confident. One thing was certain; she could not retract. If Pleasance and Rose and his settled, prosperous life here meant the most to Ives, then she must forget him, for she would not accept less than supremacy. That losing him would cause pain to her heart and her pride she could not deny, though she would get over it. She would become famous. She would be sought after. In due course she would marry advantageously, but there would be a long and weary time when all the sky was grey.

❋ CHAPTER 19 ❋

As it chanced there were various opportunities during the next few days when Ives and Lavinia could have been together. Chance favoured them for Christobel caught a heavy cold, and was so feverish and sick that her mother was considerably worried and what with helping to look after her and seeing as much as she could of Rose, who was in the restless state that comes upon some women in the last days before a birth, she had little time to wonder how Lavinia was spending her time. The Squire was always oblivious, and Owen who was concerned for Christobel but of course could not see her, was equally concerned for his sister Eliza who had been told that she and the Sisters under her, the friendless orphans and the convalescent patients, would be evicted within a fortnight.

Owen's mother wrote that poor Eliza was distracted with worry, and that nobody had been able to offer practical, helpful suggestions. It was at this juncture that Rose, who had heard the story from Christobel and had been sincerely sympathetic, made a surprising suggestion. At Derevale Manor there was the one wing which was never used nowadays, and which would have been given up to Ives and herself when they married, only that they had decided the Dower House would be preferable. Why shouldn't Owen's sister make use of it? She could bring the children for whom she had been unable to find a refuge elsewhere, and also some of the Sisters to help her. Until they could find more suitable accommodation they could all stay in the unoccupied wing. There were rooms suitable for dormitories and playrooms as well as for staff accommodation.

Owen was overwhelmed by the suggestion, and said hastily that it was impossible. The Squire would never agree and it was far too much to expect of him. Ives, for his part, was startled, as well he might be, for since her marriage Rose had cared little or nothing for anyone outside her immediate circle. It occurred to him that only extreme boredom could account for this fantastic plan having entered her head.

'I don't think Papa would object,' Rose said. 'He is very fond of children and is really kind-hearted. When the village schoolhouse had to be repaired he said the wing at Derevale could be used until the roof was sound again, and it was, for three or four months. That was long before I knew you, Ives, and it was great fun. I used to be with the village children as often as I could, and we got up to some wild pranks. Papa did not mind. It only made him laugh. Mama wasn't so pleased, for she said I was more out of hand than ever; but she's truly religious you know, and the thought of unselfish, dedicated people – nuns really – being treated so inhumanly would greatly trouble her. Papa is bound to be along to see me some time today, and I shall ask him.'

'Well, it can't do any harm to ask,' said Ives doubtfully.

To his astonishment Rose got her own way. Owen sent a telegram to his sister and received a long letter of almost incredulous gratitude. Caroline took much the line that Rose had expected her to take, and thereafter confusion prevailed.

Christobel's feverish cold yielded to treatment, but she was not allowed to rise from her bed. The maids were ordered to clean half-empty rooms, to hang curtains which Caroline unearthed from various chests stocked with linen and blankets too shabby for general use, but too good to be cast away. Derevale Manor was alert with activity. Furniture was brought down from attics, and Sister Monica wrote that necessities, such as beds and tables and also household stores would be sent by road from the Settlement.

In this upheaval Lavinia had no part whatsoever. Nothing was expected of her. It was accepted that she was easily exhausted and was too occupied with her music to have time for anything else. Elsie, Millicent, and even little Adelaide were eager to help, and for hours at a time everyone available collected in the now transformed wing of the rambling old Manor, each one with a dozen tasks allotted to them.

Ives thought of all this as a god-sent chance to meet Lavinia without attracting observation. They could be together each day for an hour or more. If it was a pleasure to make love to Rose, to make love to Lavinia was ecstasy, and as she had already willingly surrendered to him, he was perplexed and angry because she now evaded him. When she made a tryst with him she seemed half-reluctant, and she was always on the alert, insisting that it was not safe to be alone together, that although he had outwitted Christobel, he would not be so fortunate with anyone else.

Ives did not understand her, not suspect that she was capable of calculation. Lavinia had every faith in herself. She knew that her sensual attraction was great, but having shown Ives what it could be like to have her as a lover, she had now sufficient strength of will to be niggardly. Let him remember that occasion and long for its repetition. She knew better than to allow the delight she could give to become a commonplace. She would be all his again when for her sake he threw over his wife and children and Pleasance, but not before.

So Ives fretted restlessly and Lavinia stifled her own desire and was consoled by his impatience and his reproaches. She would be leaving Derevale on the day after Sister Monica and her brood arrived, and but for Ives she would have been glad to leave. The family life at the Manor bored her considerably, and it would be even worse when the place was invaded by a pack of children. In the grounds they would be underfoot, they would scream and shout, and the black-garbed Sisters, if they fraternized with the family, would be dull company at best.

Caroline and the younger girls might put up with all this, but not Lavinia.

Petulantly she told Ives as much on the day before her departure. It was necessary to see him before then, and she had sought him out in the park at Pleasance, where he was still belabouring the massive oak tree.

The trunk of the Hydra was sawn half-through, though to the casual glance this was not perceptible. Ives knew that he was the master and that through his efforts the great tree was doomed, but by some chance or peculiarity the Hydra still stood upright, showed no tendency to lean forward or sideways, and would not do so, he thought with a grudging admiration, until his axe had slashed through its entire circumference.

There would, he estimated, be hours of work on it before it would crash defeated to the ground. It was as though the great tree was a sentient being, as though it had put up a human fight against him, while satellite trees looked on, powerless to give assistance. Now he could picture how it would be when the patch of sky was no longer obscured by the wide-spreading branches and their heavy foliage. The cleared sward would be covered by the fallen Hydra, and from the many nests it had harboured the birds would rise with piercing cries. Even when the branches were cut away it would need several men to hoist the trunk upon a cart to remove it.

At first his muscles had ached intolerably at the close of a day's work, but now he had become accustomed to such strenuous exertion, and tormented as he was by Lavinia's denying tactics, he found solace in his physical strength. He was not consciously showing-off as he raised his axe on high and smote the Hydra, but he saw with satisfaction the flicker of admiration that passed across Lavinia's face.

She might be resolved to leave, might pretend coldness and put the onus of decision upon him, but she had made herself especially beautiful before seeking him out today. She had said she would visit Rose at the Dower House, and had asked for the use of the carriage which was willingly granted, but on reaching the Dower House she had told the coachman to stop before arriving at the main door, and had said casually that she would first walk over to Pleasance to see what building progress had been made during the last few days. What the man made of it when he saw her set off across the grounds, she did not pause to consider. She knew Ives would be working in the park, and if Rose questioned him later he could invent a story as good as the one he had invented for Christobel.

So now she stood there, watching him, and it crossed her mind that in breeches and open-necked shirt, with sleeves rolled to the elbows, he had never looked more handsome. His face, neck and arms were deeply tanned. In his tall, lithe body, lean-hipped but broad of shoulder, there was a stirring vitality; his thick, dark hair was damp with the heat of his exertions and clung in rings to his brow. He was the epitome of vigour and health and good looks, and he was hers, Lavinia secretly triumphed.

As for herself, she knew that the effect she made against the prevailing green of the background must be one of beauty, for she wore a light summer gown of shell pink, with a charming pretence of a bonnet – a snood of rose petals on her fair hair. Gloves and boots were both of fine white kid. The boots were an absurdity, buttoning with pearls to the ankle, pointed of toe and with narrow heels. Walking swiftly across the still unkempt lawns, she had nearly fallen as her foot caught on a hummock of turf.

At the crash of the axe the dying tree groaned, and it seemed to Lavinia that a long sigh of shivering sympathy passed through the surrounding trees. The sun had difficulty in struggling through the branches, but it shed a long ray on the space between the lovers.

'It's cold in here under the trees, though crossing the lawns it was unbearably hot,' said Lavinia. 'I would have been dreadfully scorched but for my parasol.'

Ives's amused glance rested on the white parasol, the silver knob of which she twisted in her hands. He said: 'I suppose that pretty thing might just about shield your adorable nose.'

Lavinia laughed, twirled the stem, and then with a dexterous twist of her wrist flung the parasol away from her. It landed on the far edge of the clearing. 'I certainly don't need it here,' she said.

'Come back to the house with me, if only for a few minutes,' Ives coaxed. 'You shall have a glass of wine to refresh you after your drive, and then I will walk across to the Dower House with you, for I suppose you really came here today to say goodbye to Rose.'

'And to you,' said Lavinia.

'How can you be so cruel? You need not have made these arrangements to leave. Heaven knows how long it will be before I see you again.'

'Heaven will have nothing to do with it. The length of

our separation depends on you, and how can you say you love me to distraction, and yet put bricks and mortar and a gloomy forest-like park before me?

'Have I said that I put them before you? There is Rose. Do you think it is an easy matter to cast her off?'

'Husbands have left their wives ere this. She will get over it. It won't break her heart.'

'Nor, I suspect, would it break yours if you were never to see me again.'

Lavinia smiled at him but said nothing, and in a sudden tumult of longing he cast the axe from him and went to her. He pulled her towards him and she yielded. Let him have something to remember on this their last meeting at Pleasance, was her fleeting thought; let him recall how sweet she was to hold, how soft her body and how fragrant. Let him realize that if he was being asked to give up much, it would be for a worthwhile prize. Her heart was beating more rapidly, and it was hard to present him with cool, inexpressive lips when he demanded them; and perhaps, she thought, an instant later, perhaps she had overacted, for he said: 'This is more than half a pretence to you.'

'Oh, no!' she sounded shocked. 'How can you put bricks and mortar and a gloomy forest-like park before me?'

'If I put bricks and mortar before you, you put your will before your love of me.'

'But that I have to do. You still belong to her.'

'Did you think of Rose when you let me love you – that first time?'

'No. I was quite carried away, but I resolved it should not happen again, not until we were together for always.'

With an exasperated, impatient movement he put her from him, turned away and picked up his axe.

'This is not a good place to be,' said Lavinia, 'and it was the same in the house. I felt then that I was being watched, rejected, hated. It is so today; as though we are not alone. I heard a twig crack just then, as though someone trod on it.'

Ives replied indifferently: 'There are the birds, the squirrels, possibly deer. In an overgrown place such as this there are always such sounds.' He delivered a crashing blow at the tree and cried out in a different voice, a warning voice: 'Move back, Livvy.'

Attempting to obey she found she could not. As Ives had pushed her away from him, her right foot in its pretty, foolish, useless boot had become firmly wedged in the hidden roots of a tree felled years before.

There was a sudden darkening as the great tree swayed on its base. Not yet afraid she cried plaintively: 'I can't – my foot has caught . . .'

'Pull off your shoe,' shouted Ives as he dashed towards her.

❋ CHAPTER 20 ❋

At the Dower House, Rose gazing somewhat forlornly from her bedroom window had seen Lavinia in the distance, speeding across the grounds on her way to Pleasance. It was only from this particular window that there was a clear view beyond the Dower House garden, but there was no mistaking that slender, graceful figure.

Lavinia must have called to see her, Rose concluded. But why in the world had she not realized that she would be at home on this blazingly hot morning? Perhaps she had some message for Ives. But in that case a servant would have been sent with it. Though for the last few weeks Rose had walked scarcely at all, her curiosity was now so great that she determined to make an effort.

As she threw a light but shrouding cape over her bulky body, she reflected with thanksgiving that within another fortnight at the latest the baby would be born. Then it was to be hoped there would be no more children for a few years. Walking slowly, cautiously, in sensible shoes, Rose set off for the park, knowing that Ives was certain to be there. His passion for manual labour was a puzzle to her, especially his determination to fell this particular, massive tree by his unaided effort. He had frequently talked about it lately, and almost as though he had a personal hatred for the tree – a hatred mingled with admiration. Why there was this urgency to demolish the Hydra, which must be hundreds of years old, Rose could not imagine.

She sighed as she laboured along, feeling as though all her youth had vanished, scarcely able to believe that within a few weeks she would be once again of a normal shape. Her mother had said that then Ives must be persuaded to take her away on a holiday – perhaps to Paris. That would be wonderful, thought Rose longingly.

The heat was intense, and before she was near the park, her hands and forehead were damp with sweat. The shade would be a relief, and on the return journey she would have Ives's arm to lean upon.

The Hydra stood not far within the park, and before Rose saw either Ives or Lavinia who were hidden by the trees, she heard their voices, at first muffled by the distance, but then audibly. Lavinia spoke :

'How can you put bricks and mortar and a gloomy, forest-like park before me?'

The words brought Rose to an abrupt standstill. Her heart lurched. What she had heard couldn't mean what it seemed to mean. She strained to hear Ives's reply. When she did, she recognized the pain as well as the anger in his voice. He asked a bitter question : 'There is Rose. Do you think it is an easy matter to cast her off?'

'Husbands have left their wives ere this . . .'

Ives's voice had been clear, but Lavinia's seemed to come from a far distance. There was a mist before Rose's eyes, and she might have fainted had not the child within her, as though it reacted differently to this stunning shock, flung itself against her ribs. Even so she sank almost to the ground and heard no more that was uttered.

The fallen branch of a tree cracked beneath her weight. In her ears it sounded like a pistol shot, and she dragged herself upright, and turning, stumbled away. A more aggressive woman might have confronted the faithless pair, but to Rose that was unthinkable; her one urgent, conscious hope was to escape, never again to look upon Lavinia in her fatal beauty. For of course she was beautiful, thought Rose as she half-blindly groped her way from the park. Was it because she had secretly feared Lavinia, had guessed that her fascination for Ives was greater than ever, that she had soothed herself by pretending her cousin's bloom had faded and that nobody would now look twice at her? How long had this intrigue flourished? Where and when could they have found the opportunity to meet? How was it they had managed to deceive everyone? Rose could answer none of these questions, and in her agony wondered why they should seem important.

What *was* of importance was the distance to the Dower House. Lawns and paths stretched endlessly before her, and she longed to be once more within the shelter of her home. There she could shed her heartbroken tears; there she could be alone. Stumbling, swaying, a grotesque figure, she doggedly plodded on. Once in the familiar shelter she would care nothing if she died. Death, however, had other victims, little though Rose suspected it.

Instantaneously as Ives threw down his axe and sprang to Lavinia's side, he realized that all the dark powers of the primeval world had risen up against him. It was not yet time for the Hydra to fall – yet it was falling; bringing about by some mysterious compulsion its own death, proud to revenge itself on a human enemy; triumphing even as it perished.

Ives bent to tug at Lavinia's boot, but it resisted all his strength, and the foot within might have been moulded to it. She cried out with pain as he wrenched at her leg, and then seized her round the waist jerking her violently towards him in the effort to release her.

Slowly the tree swayed, groaning in infinite agony as it tore apart its sinews. There was no other sound; only a watching stillness. Ives saw the darkness come down upon him. There was time enough. He could have leapt aside, leaving the trapped Lavinia to her fate, and she, at last understanding what that fate was to be, screamed as she gazed upwards. Despair, rage, and the humiliation of defeat passed over Ives in a mighty wave, but the possibility of desertion did not occur to him. Lavinia was now struggling frantically though vainly, and in a passion of grief and pain he threw his arms round her, pressed her face down upon his shoulder, and held her tightly. Smothering darkness preceded their last moment as the final tendons snapped and the monstrous tree hurled itself upon them.

Rose was almost at home when she heard the distant crash, and for an instant it was as though the earth rocked beneath her feet. Once more faintness overwhelmed her, and her breath came sobbingly as she clutched at the tall, wrought-iron gate which opened upon the garden path.

Across the lawns leading from the new, nearly completed Pleasance, workmen, headed by Owen Allen were running. Nearer to the park, the crash and its reverberations were stupendous, but they had no idea as yet of the tragedy brought about by the falling of the Hydra. They did know, however, that this was not according to plan. When the time came the topmost branches should have been caught by a lasso, and the great tree eased to its death. There had been talk of such a finale for the next day or the day after.

As Owen came upon the scene the birds were shrilling a lament. His gaze fell upon the towering, sprawling giant, upon the stump from which it had been torn, and then lingered upon what, half-obscured by scattered leaves appeared to be a large, white flower. He moved closer to it, and with the first throb of ghastly apprehension saw that it was a white parasol.

✻ CHAPTER 21 ✻

It took time, it took concerted labour before the great trunk of the tree was lifted and the broken bodies brought forth. Felled, they had gone down clasping each other, and although Ives's face was crushed, Lavinia's still pressed against his shoulder was unmarred.

Owen rode on horseback to Derevale Manor to break the news to the Squire and Caroline, whose concern after the first shock was all for Rose. She could not be told, yet how was it possible not to tell her? The Squire, grieved and horrified, said that this was a woman's business; only Rose's mother could now be of consolation to her. In the bewilderment, the horror-struck incredulity of the first moments, nobody wondered what had brought Lavinia to the park; she who had left Derevale in the carriage to visit Rose.

Even before holding Rose's hand and talking brokenly about a serious accident to Ives, Caroline was anxiously aware of her daughter's pinched and suffering face. But it was a great relief that Rose should be so calm. Having listened to her mother's stumbling speech, she said, faltering but without tears: 'Mama, it's worse than that, isn't it? If the great tree fell and Ives was beneath it, how can he be alive?'

It was Caroline who then sobbed aloud with her daughter's arms around her. 'Was he alone?' asked Rose.

'Oh, my darling, no. It's a double tragedy. Livvy died with him. How can I ever tell poor Hilda?'

Rose was very quiet. She mechanically stroked her mother's hair. She said at last: 'I asked, because this morning I saw Livvy walking across to Pleasance. I thought she must be in search of Ives, that she had a message for him.'

'None that I know of, my darling. But perhaps – yes, that must have been it. She was leaving us tomorrow, you know, and it may have occurred to her that it was her opportunity to bid him goodbye. Oh, poor Livvy, if only she hadn't! It is thought she was the cause of their . . . their . . . you see, my love, her foot had caught in the fissure of an old tree root. One of the men who worked to get them out discovered that and told Owen Allen. Her boot was wedged fast; they had to hack the root away to release her poor foot. Ives could have saved himself – perhaps he should have done, a married man – a father – '

'Oh, no, Mama, how could he abandon her to such a dreadful fate? He couldn't save her, but – '

'He died as a hero. You can be proud of him, Rose,' said Caroline, thinking that it was a useless heroism, as many such acts were.

'I knew he was felling the great tree,' Rose said, painfully, 'but it wasn't expected to fall today. There must have been a part of it already dead and rotten.'

And it had been so with Ives, she thought, her bitterness almost obliterating grief. She had loved him with all her being; she had borne him one child and was within days of bearing him a second; she would never have deserted him, even if illness and poverty had come upon him, but all that was of little value to him. It had been Lavinia always, though she had once been contemptuous of him, and doubtless even on this last day of their lives had exacted her own terms. She had only to smile that slow smile of hers, and gaze at him from beneath her heavy lids, and to Ives she was irresistible.

He would have gone with her, thought Rose, though he had put up a fight against it. Lavinia would have come before Pleasance, before wife and children, had it not been for the unsuspected weakness in the tree. Desperate loneliness, a heartbroken, reproachful mourning was to come later, but in the first hour of widowhood Rose was grateful to the Hydra. Now there would be no disgrace, no humiliation. Nobody would ever know. To Rose, desertion would have been a more crushing bereavement than death.

❋ CHAPTER 22 ❋

Sister Monica, her devoted colleagues and fifty-odd orphans of varying ages arrived at Derevale Manor to find a distraught family. At first to Caroline this visitation seemed the culminating disaster, but not for long. Sister Monica, tall and serene in her coif and cloak which was a blend of nurse's uniform and nun's habit, immediately grasped the situation and offered practical help which was more welcome than sympathy, though that also was given in abundance.

Rose had started in premature labour, and the midwife who had been engaged for a fortnight hence was away from the district. Sister Monica announced that she could take charge. She had midwifery as well as nursing experience and the harassed doctor, unable to find another midwife at short notice, accepted her services with thanksgiving. Within an hour of arrival, Sister Monica with a younger Sister in attendance, was at the Dower House. The others, she said equably, could settle the children into their quarters. They would be of no trouble to anyone. Her calm, her gentle capability, at once had its effect on Rose who between spasms of wrenching pain had cried out that her death was certain. And why not? What had she to live for now?

A great deal, Sister Monica told her. She was young and years of life lay before her. Within a few hours she would have two children who needed her; this little new one especially. She had her parents and her sisters who were in a sad state about her. She could not be selfish and die because she had not the will to live, thus bringing a greater sorrow upon them.

'The sorrow is all mine,' Rose moaned. 'I was the only one who really loved Ives. As for Lavinia . . .' she broke off, fearful of betraying her hatred, and ended lamely: 'We had seen very little of her for years. She was close to none of us.'

'But her poor mother will be here tomorrow, I am told,' said Sister Monica, 'and she will be in great grief. Mrs Broughton has an agonizing time before her without mourning your death. Won't you try to give some small joy to set against this tragedy; joy in your safe delivery and in the gift of your child? To give, to be allowed to give is the best thing in life.'

The last words sank deep into Rose's consciousness and were to bear a strange fruit. There were hours of pain before her, and as Caroline told Owen, she was sure that without his sister, poor, darling Rose would have sunk into a fatal stupor.

Never in after life did Rose forget that dreadful day and night, and at times she felt that the dedicated woman who helped her, consoled her and exhorted her, was wrestling for the deliverance of her soul as well as her child. For although Rose's instinct was to conceal Ives's faithlessness, in her extreme agony broken words were wrung from her which Sister Monica alone heard. Pitiful and understanding she prayed Rose to let forgiveness soften her heart. If her husband and her cousin were indeed lovers, they had met with a fearful retribution, whereas she would live to find a new happiness.

The doctor came and went, and had no idea of the undercurrent of mental agony which was harder for Rose to endure than physical pangs.

'You don't know what it means – you can't know,' cried Rose in one of the pain-free intervals when she and Sister Monica were alone together. 'You have given your love to God, and you will never be deserted.'

'But before then I gave it to a man who injured me as you have been injured,' said she whose secular name was Eliza Allen. 'We were to have been married in a few weeks, but he gave me up for another woman, who is now his wife. I have not,' she added with a wry smile, 'the satisfaction of knowing that I could have made him far happier, for he adores her and she is a good wife to him.'

'And is that why you founded this settlement?' Rose asked.

'Oh no! That happened some years later. My heart which I had thought was broken was healed by that time, and I knew that marriage would have been a mistake for me. All these children are dear to me, and how could I have the privilege of caring for them, if I had given my love to a husband? They matter so much to us all, and we have to make them believe that they matter, for then they are not orphans but just like any other happy children.'

In the early hours of the following morning, Rose gave birth to a second daughter. When she was told of it and the child was put into her arms, she was secretly glad that there was no son to grow up with a tormenting similarity to Ives in his strength and manliness and charm. The baby girl was weak and the doctor shook his head doubtfully, but Rose was sure that she would live.

'I shall call her after you,' she told Sister Monica, who in the light of day was looking wan and exhausted.

'Not Eliza, I entreat you.' The voice which had been so firm yet so gentle now shook with laughter. 'I cannot describe to you what a burden that name was for me to bear.'

'It will be Monica, of course,' said Rose, and too weary to suffer further grief, she fell into a long, dreamless sleep.

❋ CHAPTER 23 ❋

'The birth of the baby,' said Christobel, 'made it easier for Rose. I don't mean because she now has two little girls, but because she had to be looked after and couldn't share in the horror. She knows that Ives is dead and how he died, but she didn't see him – or her – and she would have insisted on it I'm sure. She doesn't know and it's to be hoped that nobody will ever tell her, that they both lay on stretchers in the great hall at Pleasance. She heard nothing about the inquest, or the stories that are floating around. I have heard them, Owen, though I wasn't intended to. It is said they were clasped together as lovers.'

'Oh, as rescuer and rescued . . . only Ives was powerless to rescue her,' retorted Owen.

'Would he have died with her if she had meant nothing to him?' Christobel wondered. 'There must have been the moment of decision, for he could have saved himself. In the open everyone calls him a hero, and praises his selfless gallantry, but I wonder if they suspect . . .'

'Nobody ever suspected him of loving Lavinia, except you, Chrissie, and you were convinced by his explanation.'

Christobel hesitated and then said: 'Not for long. I thought I would never tell you. I hoped the affair would break up when Lavinia went away, but he lied to me. Now he is dead it can't be wrong to tell you. It has been hard to bear alone, and it will be hard in the future when I hear Rose speak of him as faultless, as though he had been a perfect husband. I think it was the worry of it that made me ill. I did catch a cold, of course, but I should have shaken it off, if I hadn't been so miserable, and so afraid there was awful trouble in store for Rose. Well, of course this is trouble, but it could have been worse for her.'

'Ives convinced me as well as you,' Owen said. 'Why are you so sure he lied to us? The way they died proved nothing. As your mother says, Lavinia was leaving the next day, and when she drove over to the Dower House it was natural for her to seek out Ives to say goodbye to him. She would have been unlikely to see him again.'

'There wasn't a stain or a mark of any kind on Lavinia's green riding habit,' Christobel said slowly. 'She gave it to Ruth, Mama's personal maid, asking her to press it, after she had worn it again a few days later.'

'But Ives told you he brushed and sponged the habit,' said Owen.

'So he might have done, but it wouldn't have been perfect. I've had a toss from my pony more than once, and Mama always moaned over the mud stains. Ives couldn't have given them more than rough and ready treatment. When I was all begrimed after a fall, though Ruth did her best with my things, there were always marks and stains she couldn't get out. I stood beside her while she pressed Livvy's jacket and skirt, and I could see that what Ives said had never happened. Oh, Owen, I knew that if Livvy wanted him, poor Rose hadn't a chance.'

Owen was silent. Christobel was probably right and he pressed her hand in compassion. He thought as he had thought before, that all the trouble thrust upon her had been too much for a girl of her age. Even their own love affair, innocent though it was, had suffered, for she no longer had a child's trusting faith in the goodness of mankind.

'In some ways Rose is younger than I am,' said Christobel. 'She felt secure – never thought such a dreadful grief could come upon her; but I know, I seem to have always known that nothing in life is secure.'

'True love is, Chrissie darling.'

'Only while fate is kind.'

'No – it would endure even though one of us died. We should always remember that it had been perfect, and we shouldn't feel it was the end.'

'I wonder,' and Christobel sighed. 'Dying together sounds romantic. It has a kind of beauty. Was Livvy comforted in her last moments because Ives was with her?'

'I am sure of it. It would have been far more shocking for her had he leapt to safety. The desolation of a lifetime could have been crowded into those last seconds; but he held her, he did not let her see the tree as it crashed down on them.'

'Why did it crash – just then?' Although they were alone in the fruit garden, sitting on a bench against a sun-drenched wall where peaches ripened, Christobel instinctively lowered her voice. 'Yesterday, as you know, the men at last succeeded in taking the tree away, and curiosity – I suppose it was curiosity, for I had heard talk – made me walk across the park and look at the great stump. I thought it would surely be old and crumbling; but it wasn't. One could see what a living strength there had been, and there were still great strands and sinews attached, as though at the last it had literally torn itself away, not waited for the blows of the axe. It wasn't expected to fall as it did, was it?'

'No,' Owen admitted reluctantly. 'That has puzzled us all. But there must have been some natural reason to account for it. I wish,' he added with vexation, 'that the men had shaved the stump. I gave orders about it and thought it had been done.'

'They had no time, perhaps. I don't think it was a natural happening, but I am not surprised. When we were last there, in the park, I felt the hostility and the unrest. The Hydra was a monarch, and for Ives to bring it down by his own efforts was a kind of battle. I heard him speak of it. It excited him, but in the end the tree won and had its revenge.'

'Chrissie, I ought to scold you. That's sheer morbid fancy.'

'But I have always had fancies, though I don't know if they are morbid. All growing things have a life of their own, and to me trees are mysterious. The Hydra had stood there for centuries. There was something splendid about it. Why did Ives have the urge to destroy?'

'My dear, there's no denying that the park is overgrown, and timber is valuable and can be sold. Many of those felled trees will be used for building purposes.'

'Not at Pleasance, I hope, as it belongs to Rose. In a way it was always hers, for Papa only sold Ives the land because he was to be her husband. Now that Pleasance is almost finished, what will she do with it?'

Owen shook his head. 'I have no idea. I only know that this week Rose sent a message that the work was to go on as planned.'

'But she can't live in that great place, alone.'

'There are her children – there would be servants, and later on – Rose's life is not over, Chrissie. She may well make a second marriage. She will be a very rich woman, for I have no doubt that Ives has left her all he possessed.'

'And you think she will marry a man who will live there, instead of taking her to a home of his own?'

'Chrissie, how can I say? After all, it's her children's inheritance.'

'I suppose it is, but . . . the poor little things. They would be much happier without it. Who would want children to be brought up amongst resentful ghosts?'

'Few people are aware of the ghosts, if they exist,' said Owen.

'Oh, darling, you know that's not true. The villagers always said the grounds were haunted. Not that I think they ever saw anything, but there was the sense of oppression. Even Livvy was conscious of that. She once said so.'

Owen said regretfully: 'It's such a beautiful place. In the past the old house must have given much happiness.'

'I wonder,' Christobel said again.

CHAPTER 24

When Rose was up and out again, there were those who saw her, shook their heads dolefully, and said there was a great change in her, which was only to be expected in one widowed so young and with two orphaned children. It was a tragic sight to bring a tear to any eye. And tragedy wasn't over for her, poor young lady, said the lugubrious villagers. The infant born so soon after the father's death was very feeble and nobody expected it to survive, for all the care of the doctors and that Sister Monica, who plainly doted on the poor babe.

But after a few weeks no more was said about the baby's feebleness, for she was plainly thriving, as anyone could see who looked beneath the hood of her baby carriage. Sister

Monica still took a great interest in her namesake's welfare, though there was a middle-aged nurse for her, as well as the one who looked after little Esme. No expense spared, said the villagers, but why should there be? Mrs Tresham was very rich, and sad though she might be, rich grief was not so hard to bear as poor grief.

To her own family, Rose seemed a different being. Christobel, watching her, thought that her sister had grown up at last. Even in wifehood and motherhood she had seemed like a spoilt child, sometimes petulant, though more often good-natured and complacent and given to girlish giggles. Christobel would have dearly liked to hear again that spontaneous chuckle, but otherwise she preferred the new Rose, who was brave and patient and rarely spoke of her grief. She was thin now, as one had not supposed the plump Rose could ever be, but that had the effect of making her look even younger than her years. The black clothes she wore were plain but elegant, devoid of the fashionable mourning jewellery.

'I never guessed that Rose could be so good and unselfish,' said Caroline with wonder. 'So much of her sympathy has been for me because I had such a dreadful time with Hilda, and such anxiety over herself and the baby, let alone the grief and shock for poor Ives and Livvy. A few months ago I would not have thought I could have lived through such a terrible time.'

'Ives was a fine fellow and I liked him, but it would have been worse if Rose had been taken from us,' said the Squire to whom these remarks were addressed. 'We have much for which to be thankful. Even poor Hilda has that, for though she may never own it, Livvy was a worry to her and had been a great disappointment, and she and Rodney are happy together – much happier without a third person. Stop worrying, m'dear, about Hilda, who has a husband to fuss over her. Count your blessings. I always told you Rose was a fine girl, and had all her wits about her. To hear her talking to the lawyer is enough to surprise anyone, for finance is a ticklish business, and Ives had dozens of investments. His legal man, Norgate, is a reliable fellow and Ives must have known as much when he made him executor, but now he has taken Rose's measure and is treating her as a partner, which is more than Ives ever did.'

'Whatever makes you say that?' questioned a surprised Caroline. 'The poor boy thought the world of her.'

'In his way, but it struck me that Rose had a rival in Pleasance. To Ives she was more of an amusing toy, a pretty plaything, and to my mind that held her back. She loved him, and if that was the way he wanted her to be, she wouldn't let go against him. Not that this was conscious on her part.'

'Will she be very rich?' asked Caroline, somewhat surprised at her husband's perception. 'I have hardly liked to ask before. It seemed indelicate.'

'She'll have more than she can do with, and only two girls to rear – not such an expense as bringing up a boy; though so far as that goes she'd be a rich woman even if she had a large family to provide for. Ives left every penny to her except for one legacy.'

'Someone in America?' Caroline asked. 'He had nobody belonging to him here.'

'Nor there either it seems. No – it's young Owen Allen who benefits, and Norgate has already been in touch with him. Ives left him ten thousand.'

'But, Martin, how extremely odd. Ives liked him I know, but after all Owen was no more than a person he employed.'

'Well, it seems he thought more of him than that, and whether Ives had a notion that he would die before his time nobody knows. He made his will after wedding Rose, and this legacy to Owen was a codicil added only a few months ago. It was worded in a peculiar way. Rose told me after Norgate told her. Ives instructed that if he was still alive when Owen married, the legacy was cancelled, for he'd give him the same sum for a wedding gift. But if he died while Owen was still single the ten thousand was to be looked upon as such a gift . . . to set him up in life and to make him acceptable as a suitor to his bride's family.'

'Owen is a likeable, worthy and clever young man,' Caroline said, 'and he would surely be acceptable to most families. Not that I had any idea he was engaged. He must be, I suppose, and Ives was in his confidence.'

'Yes, he was. Rose says so. My dear, I don't know how you will take this, and you've had enough shocks, but you'll have to know. Owen is most loath to upset you further, but it seems that he and Chrissie . . . well, there's been an attachment for a year or more.'

'Chrissie! But a year ago she was only a child.'

'She was seventeen or as near to it as makes no matter, and many a girl has been married at that age.'

'Rose was more than a year older and you thought her too young, though Ives was such a good match for her.'

The Squire shrugged, too lazy to argue with his wife or to point out that his fear for Rose had been that through a harmless escapade she might be pushed into marriage. He had been wrong. His poor girl had doted on her American husband, and Ives, probably, had been equally in love with her.

'Even with ten thousand the same cannot be said of Owen,' Caroline went on. 'I know I praised him just now, and said he would be an acceptable suitor to most parents with a daughter to marry, but I was not thinking of our family. Owen's people are thoroughly respectable, but they are in trade – or were. Married to him, Chrissie would have an inferior position.'

'Oh, come now, m'dear. Originally the Broughtons were mercers, and if there's any fine breeding it is on the distaff side. You stepped down yourself when you married me. We Broughtons can't boast of so much as a knight, but there were titles enough in your family.'

'As though it's of any consequence!'

'Then why should Owen's respectable background be of consequence? He's a fine young fellow and clever beyond the ordinary. There have been architects in our family before – ancestress Linnet's father you remember. Aren't we all proud of that link?'

'I can see you are in his favour,' Caroline said. 'And so what can I do or say? All that you say of Owen is true, but I hope Chrissie knows her own mind.'

The Squire chuckled. 'You can be sure of that. She's a serious-minded young woman. Don't forget, m'dear, that you have three more daughters to marry off, and by the time you've made a match for one, you'll have the next treading on her heels.'

As though she ever forgot it, thought Caroline. That anxiety had been there almost at the birth of each new baby girl. She smiled, thinking that after all though Christobel was beautiful, she was too dreamy, too impractical to appeal to all men. Many would be driven to impatience by such a wife, but never Owen who had gentle, considerate ways and a kind heart. It was singular that she had not noticed there was more than a casual friendliness between them, though her husband said they had been in love for more than a year. Chrissie had certainly been very sly, thought Caroline with some resentment.

Later, Christobel with Owen's ring on her finger, heard her mother telling all and sundry that the family were so happy over the engagement, ending with the invariable sighing remark that she was thankful there was cause for *some* happiness after the double tragedy that had been such a dreadful blow to them all, and had wrecked poor Rose's life.

'Mama will soon believe she threw us together and hoped for this,' Christobel remarked to Owen. 'Not that it matters, for I believe she really is glad, now that she has made up her mind to it. I have Ives to thank, and I wish I had liked him better. No doubt I should have done, if I had guessed he had planned to make our marriage easy.'

'He was always extraordinarily generous,' said Owen. 'Of course I had no idea. He never hinted at it, though I know he was in sympathy with us.'

'With you – not with me. Ives only barely liked me, possibly less than I liked him. But I misjudged his kindness, for there was something imaginative and unselfish in such a gift. Even if death took him, and why he should have seemed to half expect that, I can't think, he wanted everything to come right for you. At least he knew that what you feel for me is real.'

'Yes, he knew that,' Owen agreed.

'Poor Ives. He wasn't clever at understanding women. He may have understood Lavinia, but not Rose. He perpetually underrated her. Papa is not a clever man but he didn't make that mistake.'

'Rose was too young when she married, too young in her nature.' Owen uttered the last words swiftly, aware of Christobel's even greater youthfulness. 'Some characters develop later, and we can all see how it is with Rose. Grief gave her maturity overnight, that and being the mother of a second child.'

'I don't think the second baby had anything to do with it, Owen. There are lots of feathered-headed women with large families. Grief might – and of course poor Rose is still grieving deeply, but now and again just lately, I've wondered if she knew or strongly suspected about Livvy.'

'How could she? You are the only one who suffered suspicion; mine was forgotten after Ives had given us an explanation, and you certainly did not tell her.'

'Nothing would have induced me to do that, but Rose may have guessed – something may have warned her or perhaps some carelessness. It does strike me there's something unusual in her grief; a kind of reserve, and in my hearing she has never once spoken of Livvy. It's as though Rose wants to blot her out of memory, or feels that if she did speak of her, she would be so bitter she would betray herself to us all. Oh, darling, it must be dreadful when a wife finds that her husband has put another woman before her.'

Owen took her in his arms, and kissed her, comforted her. 'That will never happen to you, my love.'

Rose, when she considered her sister's engagement, was conscious not of jealousy but of a saddened realization that Ives had never given her a quarter of such love. She spoke of it to Sister Monica, the only person to whom she could speak with perfect freedom. The bond between them was strong, for Rose knew that it was the other woman's will that had held her back from death when she would have gladly died.

'I thought he loved me enough, and I loved him crazily,' she said. 'He liked making love – we were suited in that way, though I suppose it's shameless to speak of it. My mother says that that side of marriage is distasteful to any refined woman, so I can only suppose I am not refined. It's a comfort to me to remember we at least shared something.'

'It *should* be a comfort,' said Sister Monica. 'I am not in agreement with your mother over that point, spinster though I shall always be.'

'You don't seem like a spinster, but more as though you're the mother of an enormous family. With my two babes I feel a novice. Your children are so happy. All these sad weeks I have enjoyed being with them. They gave me something to think about other than myself.'

'They *are* happy,' Sister Monica agreed. 'Of course they sometimes quarrel and they are all naughty occasionally, but I like to think they are never naughty because they are miserable. They have been especially happy since we came here. Your mother in all her distress and worry has been so good to them. We tried to keep them quiet, and there was a strict rule that they were not to stray beyond the enclosed garden which belongs to the wing that has been so kindly lent to us. But your mother said they were to play in the shrubbery and other parts of the grounds, and she insisted that the noise they made didn't worry her. Then too, you and all your sisters have joined in their games and sung their little hymns with them.'

'I thought that for children brought up in a religious community there would be far more hymns,' said Rose candidly, 'and prayers too. With you there is no more than we had as children.'

'It would be a pity if one overloaded their young minds and made them dislike what should be their happiness. There is no greater joy than to love one's Creator. They do realize that already, or most of them do, and find it very easy to be grateful because they have been given this wonderful holiday.'

Rose looked at her thoughtfully. She said: 'A holiday sounds so brief, so impermanent. I know my parents wanted you to stay here for as long as you wished. Having the other Sisters and the children is no inconvenience for them, for it is really as though you all lived in a separate house.'

'Such a refuge has been the greatest help to us,' Sister Monica assured her, 'and it is of course a personal joy to me to be able to see my brother frequently. Few things could have made me happier than his engagement to your sister. She is beautiful and unusual; they care so much for each other, and I would say are well suited. My family are most anxious to meet her. I believe your mother has promised to take her on a short visit before the wedding.'

'Owen and Chrissie want it to be a quiet one,' said Rose, 'otherwise they would have to wait a year before the family are out of mourning. Pleasance will be finished before then. Owen is proud of it, for it is largely his creation, but I think he is wise to decide to live in London when they are married. If a man is ambitious it is the best centre.'

'Will you live at Pleasance?' asked Sister Monica.

Rose answered evasively: 'I want to see it finished. It soon will be. The roof is one; the glass is in all the windows. I am planning to sell the land which has been let out for ages, and the park, I think, will also be sold. It is so separated from the house that Pleasance will be little diminished by the loss of it. Chrissie is glad, for she says that what happens to the trees will then be none of our responsibility. Probably it will remain much as it is, for I know Sir John Merrilees is interested, and he is called an eccentric because of his love of birds and all wild life. He has long wanted to acquire some such park as a bird sanctuary. It is the great interest of his life, and the poor man needs some such interest with his wife dead and both his girls about to be married. For me it would be a happy solution.'

'It would certainly mean,' said Sister Monica, 'that the beauty of the landscape was preserved. This does not seem to be a part of the world where many new houses are built.'

'There is no pressing need for them. We are not densely populated, and even with the new railways being laid in all directions, I doubt if there will ever be a branch line very near. We are off the beaten track. Is that a disadvantage for your settlement?'

'On the contrary. It is an advantage; the children thrive in the pure, good air, and the country produce is so much cheaper. It may be out of the way for the work-worn women to whom in the town we could offer rest and care, but that was never more than a minor part of our activities. However, I suppose it will be our fate after this respite to start again in a crowded town. My eldest brother has written to say that he thinks he can make arrangements for us to rent what was once a large warehouse. We could have it on a long lease, but we should have to raise considerable funds to convert it into a reasonable dwelling-place.'

Rose said thoughtfully: 'I suppose in some ways – taking a long view – it would be easier to place these children in suitable situations in a city?'

Sister Monica was uncertain: 'I have given much thought to that, and I can only say that I don't know. Their first youth is so important. Our eldest children are only six or seven years of age. I have such dreams – impractical perhaps – of allowing them to develop their personalities. Even while so young you can see their capabilities forming. Many of these little girls will be happy in domestic service, but some have a different capacity, and by the time they are grown there may be very different opportunities for women. I only wish our children could be taught at home, instead of attending outside schools, for some of our Sisters are gifted as teachers. Sister Felicity for one is a clever woman with a gift for languages. But to establish a really good school would need much organization, and spacious quarters, let alone considerable expenditure. We shall never be more than a small settlement, and can take other children only as our odd-fifty grow up and leave us. But even to give fifty girls a chance in the world, to send them out well educated, with high principles as well as sturdy bodies built on good food and fresh air, is something.'

'It is a great deal,' said Rose soberly. 'I want to help you.'

'But so you have, my dear. I had not believed that any one family could be so kind, so generous, much though charitable people have done for us in the past. Many are inclined to think that my ideas are impossible. They do not believe that an orphanage can be a real home, but we know it can, because we have so much love to give. My hope is that in days to come our children will look back on happiness, and I pray they will always keep in touch with us; visit us, and bring their children to see us.'

'Could you be happy to make their home and yours, here for always?' Rose asked.

For once Sister Monica was startled out of her serenity. 'But that would be an unwarrantable imposition, my dear. Your parents could not be expected to consent to it, and the obligation on our side would be great. There can be too much acceptance, Rose. It can fret one's spirit.'

'I was not thinking of my parents, but of myself – and Pleasance,' Rose said. 'I have been thinking of it for weeks. That has done me good and has distracted my mind from my troubles. I am attached to you so much.' She broke off to ask: 'Can I drop the formal Sister?'

The older woman laughed. 'Of course. You can call me Eliza if you wish, much as I have always detested my name.'

'Oh no, it must be Monica. We shall probably call the baby Vonnie, as little Esme does. These childish names stick. Please, dear Monica, if we can arrange this, and there is no reason why we shouldn't, for I have already consulted my lawyer, do not feel that acceptance is too much. Did you not save my life?'

'If I did, it was because God gave me the power, and intended it should be saved, or rather that you should be helpful to save yourself.'

'Then it must have been for some purpose, and through you I have the opportunity to do real good. I could never live at Pleasance. It is too large and at present the thought of it alone is pain. But I should soon forget that if you were established there; if it became your settlement, and a happy home for so many. You could have your school, Monica, and Mr Norgate, my lawyer, says it is possible to set up a trust fund of some kind, or is it an endowment? I have listened to so much legal talk lately that I get confused, for all that he is kind and compliments me on my clear head. But what it means is that every year there would be a sum for basic necessities at least, and for the rest there would be the voluntary subscriptions which have always been your mainstay.'

The older woman looked dazed. Elation, gratitude, thanksgiving were all subdued by a note of doubt. She said: 'I did not realize that Pleasance was unconditionally yours.'

'But it is. With the exception of Owen's legacy, Ives left all he possessed to me.'

'But you have your children to consider. In years to come

they might greatly resent your action.'

'If so, they will be excessively greedy, for they will have large dowries, and when I die they will be rich women. You look almost frightened, Monica, but there's no need. Mr Norgate says there will have to be trustees, but while you live, whether or not you retire from active supervision, Pleasance will be your home. No doubt the scheme will grow and expand in ways which we cannot now foresee. When you talk to Mr Norgate, he will explain better than I can.'

'But does he think you should do that?'

'Oh, yes. He is a very good man and says that yours is a noble work, and that mine will be a worthy action. It will give me a great interest. I am full of energy, and the two little girls and looking after a house would not be enough to entirely fill my life.'

'You may marry again, Rose.'

'Never. That has been said before today, though with hesitation because Ives has been dead for so short a while; but I know within my heart that I shall stay as I am. I loved too much, trusted too much and was deceived so easily. Another man would have a very bad time with me, for I should distrust without cause.'

Her friend did not contradict her. It might be so, but none could foretell the future, not even a disillusioned young widow. Sister Monica was dazed by the magnitude of the scheme, but Rose went on persuasively: 'If you refuse I cannot imagine what will happen to Pleasance. For myself, I am satisfied with the Dower House, and should much dislike to let or sell Pleasance to a stranger. The houses are too near each other. But I could not leave it empty for years on end.'

'I would not dare to refuse,' said Sister Monica simply. 'It is more than I ever longed for.'

CHAPTER 25

Rose, in the role of Lady Bountiful was approved by her relations and all who knew her, with the exception of Christobel. She was inclined to think that Rose, though intending to be generous and doubtless benevolently inclined towards the orphans and the adult members of the Community, was in truth ridding herself of an encumbrance.

'Yes – well, so I am,' Rose admitted. 'I don't pretend otherwise. I was proud of Pleasance while it was being rebuilt because it was Ives's pride. We should have had a very full social life, or at least that was what he first planned.' She faltered for a minute and then went on: 'That would have worked out very well, and with guests coming and going, Pleasance would not have been too large. Besides, I don't expect our family would have stopped at two girls. But now it is all different. It is only sensible to make use of that great place, and it will commemorate Ives's memory. I want him to be known as the Founder. There will be a plaque engraved and put up over the front entrance to say so.'

'Children should have a happier home in which to grow up,' said Christobel stubbornly.

'But in the ordinary way our children would have grown up there,' Rose pointed out.

'Well – yes – because it would have been their family home, and your two girls might not have noticed anything disagreeable or frightening; but for an orphanage or a school it seems anything but suitable.'

'But, Chrissie, it's a beautiful house. For me it has unhappy associations, but otherwise . . . oh, there's nothing wrong with it. You only imagine that it's haunted.'

Christobel shrugged helplessly. How could one argue with Rose, who had set her heart on this scheme? The younger girl could visualize terrified children who might come under the spell of a malign influence. But who would take her fear seriously?

Perturbed, Christobel left the enclosed Dower House garden, and wandered across the lawns to Pleasance, which was now ready for occupation. The existing settlement furniture would need to be much amplified, and already there was a van from the nearest large town standing outside the main entrance. Dining-room furniture was being moved in; very different furniture from that which Ives would have bought for his own use. But Christobel readily admitted that it would have been ridiculous to have anything but long tables and plain chairs for a school.

Suddenly she was struck by a sense of emptiness. The atmosphere to which she had become accustomed had been expectant, if not exactly hostile, but today there was nothing; no consciousness of being watched, no suggestion of the past triumphing over the present. The voices of the men moving in the furniture echoed through empty rooms. Pleasance could have been any new house, large or small, which had not yet received an imprint from occupation. That so bewildered her that she was unaware of another presence until Sister Monica touched her shoulder. Then Christobel jumped.

'As though I had run a pin into you,' said Sister Monica. 'What is it, my dear? You looked as though – well, as though you had never been here before.'

'Perhaps I haven't,' said a dazed Christobel.

'You were in a dream. How very nice the dining-room will look. Space is so important for children.'

'It's all different,' said Christobel, wondering if she could make herself intelligible to this Eliza Allen who liked to be called Monica, and who would soon be her sister-in-law. 'I wasn't a bit happy about you and Pleasance. Starting up a school here, I mean.'

'Why not, Chrissie?'

'It's too old. I mean the foundations are. It belongs to the past, and children are the present and the future.'

Sister Monica said: 'I have heard stories about the old Pleasance. The ruins and the grounds were supposed to be haunted. The villagers would not come near them after dark. Then there was the tragedy in the park which had its curious aspects, and your mother told me that you had an odd experience.'

'I did – it was frightening, but fascinating. I've never forgotten it. And since then I've often felt . . . oh well, I could rarely nerve myself to be here alone. There *are* ghosts – '

'Poor things,' said Sister Monica. 'I wonder why they have clung to this earthly habitation for so long.'

'They loved it too well,' said Christobel earnesly. 'They sinned for it, and sacrificed for it – but that's not the whole of it. It can't be, for the lady I saw when I was a child must have been Eloise Pallistier and she hated it here.'

'Perhaps,' said Sister Monica, 'they were afraid of moving on to another place of which they knew nothing. They may have been unsure of their welcome.'

'That's not orthodox religion.' Christobel gazed at the fine, gentle face with lively interest. 'We're told that when we die we go to heaven – and I suppose there are some people who believe in hell, though I don't. It's all confused, for we're also told that we shall arise from our graves at the Last Trump, which seems to suggest that we scurry back to them from heaven or from wherever we have been in the meantime.'

Sister Monica said : 'Many things taught about the after-life can be made to sound comical. My own feeling is that one should not be too literal. One thing alone is clear – that when we leave this world it is to be with God, though perhaps the law of free-will still operates, and there are those who hold back for a while. But, Chrissie, this beautiful house, and the equally beautiful grounds are now dedicated to making God's children good and happy, and no shade from the past will want to frighten trustful and happy children. If any of those old spirits feel impelled to return for a while, to look at the scenes where they once lived, then I am sure they will be tender to the children and not allow them to be aware of it.'

'Perhaps they won't want to return,' said Christobel hopefully, 'for when I stood here and looked around, just before you came in, it all felt empty – swept and garnished and waiting for new impressions.'

'I know.' Sister Monica smiled contentedly. 'We have

been given a wonderful present, and as we are all uplifted about it, and are more grateful than I can express to the Creator and to Rose who must have been divinely inspired, it certainly couldn't be spoilt for us by a ghostly hostility. You see, dear, we do sincerely love each child that we are able to care for. Often it expresses itself in very practical ways, such as Sister Laura's puddings – she is happy when we have a large stock of jam and she can use more than is strictly necessary for rolypoly – and Sister Joan loves to brush the children's hair and make it shine, and I am especially happy when I see the older girls caring for the little ones, when I hear them laughing and watch them at work or play. It's all so simple, Chrissie. We usually enjoy every moment of the day from dawn to eve, and we are grateful because of it. Nothing will hurt the Sisters or our dear children. As time passes, you will see.'

'I see already,' said Christobel. 'You are right. I shan't worry about you any more. I shall be selfish and think of my trousseau and my wedding and of darling Owen.'

Sister Monica put her arm round her and kissed her. Believing herself to be a very fortunate but very ordinary person, she had not the least idea that to Christobel the aura of absolute, selfless goodness had for a moment seemed visible; a clear, pale halo about Monica's neatly-capped head. This could, Christobel felt obliged to admit, have been caused by the way the light was shining through the mullioned window in the hall, or it could have been due to her own active imagination, but even so, it was a beautiful moment and to Christobel a moment of truth.